BIGAMIST

Elaine FLOWERS

Published by:
Before You Publish — Book Press
Addison, Texas

Edits & Cover Designs:
In House at Before You Publish — Book Press

Published and printed in the United States of America
Copyright © 2018 Elaine Garcia

First Edition
ISBN-13: 9780974738833

Printed in the United States of America

Flowers, Elaine
BIGAMIST — First Edition

BIGAMIST

Elaine FLOWERS

BeforeYouPublish Book Press™
——— We Publish Books ———
ADDISON, TEXAS

In memory of one of the best storytellers
I know and one of my biggest fans,
Aunt Johnnie Mae Carter.

It meant everything when she said
she loved reading my work.

One

Rose McDaniel

...on our way back to happy.

*P*eople become addicted to many things. It's not really the *thing*; it's the feeling they get from the thing they're addicted to. The feeling of comfort you get from biting into something deep-fried with melted cheese and bacon on top. The rush from buying a cashmere sweater for five dollars that was once one hundred dollars. The feeling an addict has of being in control of everything when snorting cocaine. The carefree feeling drunks have when vodka flows through their veins.

Love is an addiction.

I was addicted to the feeling of being in love. Not just when love was new, but I craved the butterflies every time Rick said or did something to let me know I was his world. Every time he made me feel like there was no one, not even his patients (even though I knew it wasn't true) that came before me. There was a warm sensation that started out in the pit of my stomach and when it moved to my chest, butterflies replaced it. After a few seconds, I'd be lightheaded. I felt high. It was wonderful.

Rick, on the other hand, was addicted to people falling and being in love with him. So, we were a natural pair—and a natural disaster.

I'm going to start this as close to the beginning of the end as I can remember.

We were gone a week.

To our surprise, unseasonable frost rested on the grass and mailbox when the Towne car pulled into our circle drive to deliver us home sweet home. Monday mornings were always my favorite time. I lived for beginnings—fresh starts, like morning, a new day, and the marking of a new week. So, Monday mornings were two in one—they still are.

Despite the chill in the air, this Monday was no different. I shivered, pulled my lightweight wrap snuggly about my shoulders, stepped out, and raced to the front door. Rick and the driver handled the baggage.

I made a big deal out of our anniversary every year. This year, Rick and I flew to Cozumel to celebrate. It may not sound like a big deal for the average couple but there were two reasons it was a big deal for us. One, as workaholics, we enjoyed few things more than work. And two, since I had an aversion to civil unions and refused to actually accept Rick's many marriage proposals, we didn't celebrate an anniversary in the traditional sense, so I owed him some time away to make up for that.

We'd been 'happily together' for eleven years and even if I wanted to change my mind about getting married, I was afraid of jinxing things with a formal ceremony. Every time he asked for my hand and I'd say no, I felt bad for a few days and then I'd hear of one of our friends getting divorced, and soon after, I'd get over it.

"What time do you have to check in?" Rick yelled over his shoulder as he carried the suitcases down the hall to our room.

I stood in the kitchen in front of the stove debating on whether to turn on the kettle for tea or to start the coffeemaker. I didn't have to ask him because he'd take whatever I served him. He was easy like that.

"Not until tomorrow but I'll probably head over this afternoon." I turned the fire on beneath the kettle. "You?"

"As much as I hate to cut our vacation short," Rick's voice moved closer, "I have two being dismissed today."

I gave him a disapproving look and said, "There you go trying to one-up me." We stared at each other for a moment before giving the other a competitive smile. "Have tea with me before you leave." I removed two teacups from the cabinet, placing them on the counter. "And there's eggs, too." I pointed toward the fridge.

I felt Rick's lean body standing behind me. His cinnamon-colored arms, just starting to show signs of aging on his 57-year-old body, rested on the counter on either side of me. He was aging gracefully. Even the silver hairs on his chest were now revealing what the hair on his head will be in the coming years. The front of his hard body pressed up against the back of mine as he tightly squeezed me.

"I'm about to rid myself of airplane germs." His lips pressed up against my neck. "You can join me if you like."

"Maybe... After I go through some of this mail." I pointed at a huge pile in a basket on the kitchen

9

desk that our neighbor was asked to bring in daily while we were away.

Rick looked toward the basket. "I doubt I'll be in the shower long enough for you to go through all of that." He planted another kiss. "Come on."

The warmth from the rays coming through the skylight above us was taking the chill from the room as rapidly as the warmth coming from Rick's touch. I turned and snuggled up against him. "I guess one more time to officially end our anniversary is called for. Who knows when we'll be able to indulge like this again."

Rick removed my wrap and we kissed. All week we'd been all over each other like we had when we first met. April 13th, the day we met, was usually when we got away to commemorate.

Rick was nothing like the men I was normally attracted to. His classic good looks and straight-laced-everything-by-the-book attitude was nothing like I would've even considered before. Not to mention, he was a nerd — and had the typical god-complex that most surgeons had. Not my type at all. Also, where I believed that the body could mostly heal itself, he was ready to cut it open at every opportunity.

"Hurry up," he said as he turned and headed toward our master suite.

I reduced the heat under the kettle to low, pulled out a stick of African Violet incense and lit it, and then peeked quickly inside the basket. My plan was to shuffle through the few on top while waiting on the scent to keep Rick and I in a good space, to fill the room. There were our normal credit card and utility bills, flyers, sales papers, and other junk mail. I kept going only to discover, mixed in the clutter, a bill I didn't recognize. The Plastic Surgery Center of

Texas addressed to Dr. Erick Hart. One swift swipe
with a letter opener and the seal was broken. The
paper slid out and I quickly scanned the front page.

Date: Wednesday February 21, 2018
Surgeon: Sylvester Cole, MD
Patient: Amy M. Hart
Cosmetic Procedures: Rhytidectomy,
Blepharoplasty, Skin Resurfacing
Total Bill: $10,737.37
Provider: $7,500.00
Amount Due: $3,237.37

This was not the first time I'd run across one of
his ex-wife's bills. I knew there were certain things
he felt obligated to take care of for her, but this was a
bit much. I had nothing against the woman, in fact,
she and I had only seen each other a few times in all
the years Rick and I had been together. I'd spent
some time with their kids but even that didn't
happen often. They were college-age now, and in the
beginning, I thought they just didn't want to be
around us—or maybe just a little salty about the
divorce, and all. I figured if I agreed to make things
legal, I would feel more empowered to ask him to
bring them around. It was just as well; I grew up in
the foster care system, never having a family of my
own, so I wasn't crazy about trying to build one.
Plus, his children were older and it became just too
awkward.

When I stepped into the bedroom, there was a
trail of his clothes on the floor, so I added to them
and shed my own. I removed the wrap around my
head and my golden-brown locks fell to the middle
of my naked back. My bare feet padded across the
bathroom floor and I tugged open the shower door

to find Rick covered from head to toe in shampoo and soapsuds.

"Hey, baby," he said and stepped face first under the warm spray of water. "You almost missed out." He grabbed me by both arms, pulling me in close.

With getting back to the business of daily life on our minds, the luxury of timelessness that vacationing provides was slipping away. Despite that, Rick and I embraced and kissed as the water poured down onto us both. We enjoyed each other's bodies and then lathered up with soap.

"Hey, a bill came for Amy... mixed in with the mail."

"What?"

"For cosmetic surgery." I tried to ignore the flinch in his countenance. "Why would you be getting her bill?"

"I don't know—I'll take care of it." Rick moved to the back of the shower and stood behind me. He didn't like conflict.

"You'll take care of it, meaning you're paying it?" I knew he hated to argue, and who didn't? But I couldn't help but ask. Too many times I didn't, but eyelifts and all her other white woman shit she had done to her face needed to be addressed if he was footing the bill. I honestly had nothing against her. How could I? She'd never caused any problems where Rick and I were concerned, and I appreciated that.

"That's not what I meant, but since when has it been an issue for me to take care of some of her bills?"

I stepped under the spray of water under my own showerhead and watched suds slide down the drain.

"A facelift? That hardly seems like it should be our responsibility. If she wants elective surgery, that should be on her dime." I opened the shower door and stepped out. "But you do what you wanna do." He always did...

Rick stepped out behind me. "Look, I have to go to Sherman later in the week, so I'll talk to her and handle it. It's possible that the bill accidentally came here."

I wrapped my torso in a sage-colored bath towel and then handed him an extra-large one, watching as he ran it across his chest and arms. I moved to my side of the bathroom and left him to his. "Look, I've never had a problem with you making sure the mother of your children isn't suffering but it's been eleven years." I took a seat at the vanity counter. "Your kids are off on their own, so I just don't think you should be as involved as you are with her."

With our backs facing one another, Rick was in front of his sink preparing to shave.

"I know we're not married — legally, anyway. And I admire the amicable relationship you have with her, I really do... it's just that..." I looked around for my body cream and remembered it was still packed in the suitcase. I spotted a bottle of lotion and pumped some out into the palm of my hand. "You know what... forget I said anything."

"I said I would handle it." The tone he used was humdrum, almost robotic. He turned on the water and a buzzing razor scraped lightly across his face.

"I know, and I'm sure you will." I spread the lotion over one leg, and then rubbed it in. "I'm sorry."

"Nothing to be sorry about."

"You never said if you wanted breakfast?" And just like that, I let it go. The incense fragrance wafted

13

through to the bathroom and we were on our way back to happy.

Two

Iris Hart

...I took in the love...

"They're ready for you." A broad-shouldered nurse looked around the small waiting room that was separated from the larger one I started out in. "Is he still not here?"

I glanced at the screen of my phone even though I knew there was no new message. I then held it up in the air. "He said he was exiting 45 more than five minutes ago." There was pleading in my voice when I said, "I'm sure he's going to walk in any moment."

"Why don't we just start prepping you? They'll keep a look out and send him back." She stretched out a hand, inviting me back. "This way."

I finished my status update:

```
About to see my baby
again ☺ Pics coming
soon! #sonogram
```

Post.

I tossed my phone inside my Michael Kors bag and used all of my strength to stand to my feet. This was completely different than the last time, which made it clear we were having a boy this go around.

I waddled into the room and the two technicians were on standby, waiting on me to plop my sluggish body up and onto the table. It was just as well that we got started because my bladder was about to burst from all the water I had been instructed to drink.

"He should be here in just a moment." I placed my purse in the chair next to the door and sat upright on the table with some help. "He missed the last time by just a few minutes and I would hate for him to—"

There was a light knock on the door just before it opened. The receptionist poked her head in. She then stepped back so Erick, who was still wearing his surgical scrubs, could rush in.

"I didn't miss anything, did I?"

"Hi, honey." I held out a hand in his direction and laid back onto the table.

"No, we're just about to start." The broad-shouldered woman picked up a bottle of warm gel and scooted in close to the table.

Erick stood next to me, holding my hand, and then leaned in for a quick kiss.

"Sorry." He kissed me again.

"Just glad you made it this time."

After the warm gel landed onto my taut skin, she gently pressed the transducer there and moved it around.

Erick's face lit up when the image appeared on the monitor. "There's my boy," Erick spoke lowly but the excitement and pride were apparent. He kissed me again and rubbed my arm.

When he called that morning saying that he had an early surgery scheduled, I was afraid that meant he wouldn't make it. It had happened so many times

16

before. I had already made peace with us not arriving at the doctor's office together as we had planned—and as he'd promised. There were lots of broken promises with Erick but never any that really mattered. He was away for a week at a medical conference, which was the reason we rescheduled the sonogram for today. When he returned the day before, he had patients that he needed to see so he ended up being at the hospital all night. He loved his patients in a way that was difficult for me to accept at times. But that wasn't new information. When his text came in saying he was on his way, I was so relieved. He'd missed so much.

"Nice strong heartbeat..." The technician scanned every area on my swollen belly it seemed. "...kidneys, liver, lungs—all looks good—right on schedule for 29 weeks. He's almost at five pounds."

We both peered at the screen, anxious for more details.

"I just emailed you both a photograph. Do you want me to print one too?"

"Yes, thank you so much," I said. The machine gave a light buzz and she stood and wiped the gel off my still exposed abdomen.

The image of our son on a piece of photo paper slipped out of a printer across the room. The technician took it as soon as it hit the tray and waved it around as if it was a Polaroid. She then placed it near my handbag.

"I'll put this here, and we'll meet you both out front."

Erick kissed my swollen belly and tugged my Juicy Couture top over it. "Have you had lunch?"

"Not yet." I sat up and swung my legs over to one side. "Jersey has to be picked up shortly, so..."

"Let's get her now, and then grab a bite," he said while helping me to my feet.

I was so relieved he didn't have to rush off. The three of us, soon to be four, didn't spend enough time together but when we did, it was good. Always. That had something to do with the fact we didn't spend enough time together for it to ever be bad. I hated it when I thought like that—like my mother—but it certainly made me wonder. Every time we were together it was like a holiday, a fiesta. It was a celebration and Erick treated his girls well to make up for his frequent absences. I was afraid, as my mother so analytically pointed out, if he were around more often, there would be no fiesta. Jersey and I would no longer be special. That would then be the end.

"Before I can think about food, I have to pee. I am seriously about to drown over here." I tossed the photo into my bag and carried it out of the room.

"I'll meet you up front," Erick said as he fell in behind me.

I busted through the door of the unisex restroom, locked the door, and planted my spreading behind on the toilet. I gave up trying to straddle public toilet seats at six months. My equilibrium had been jacked up the whole pregnancy. I'd tripped and fallen more carrying this boy than I had in my whole life. So, I sat. Knowing I was in for at least a three-minute leak, I dug into my purse and pulled out my phone. I turned the sound on and alerts dinged one after the other.

I scanned through the comments and decided to go ahead and snap a shot of the ultrasound pic.

Share.

    I can't wait to meet
    my growing boy! <3

Post.

Instantly, several comments and hearts and thumbs-up icons calculated. I took in the love, smiled, and finished my business. But before I walked out:

```
On  my  way  to  lunch
with the hubster!
```

Post.

Every day I craved a grilled chicken salad from Firehouse Grill so that was where I demanded we go. We placed a booster chair next to Erick, but his lap was Jersey's preferred seat. She was back and forth between his lap and standing next to him with her arms noosed around his neck.

"Why don't you make her sit?" I asked Erick while holding my glass up for the waitress to refill my iced tea.

"She's fine." He kissed the top of her head. "I thought we talked about the artificial sweeteners."

I slid the two yellow packets back into the holder on the table and picked up four sugar packets.

"And didn't I hear you ask for sweet tea?"

My phone was dinging with new alerts.

"It's not sweet enough," I said and sighed. I then tossed the sugar packets back as well. "Are you coming home tonight—the roof guy came the other day—he said we need the whole thing replaced—we need to hire another company for the lawn." I touched the screen on the front of my phone.

"Can you put that thing away for just a minute? Damn." Erick hated my social interactions. He made it clear that he didn't want me discussing him online. He said that he was a high-profile surgeon and it wasn't a good idea for him to be so public. I guess I understood that. It wasn't like he needed to advertise his skills.

19

"Sorry..." I said and then quickly...
Check In:

```
Having my favorite
meal at the Firehouse
Grill-love it! #yummy
```

Post.

"Okay, what was I saying?" I looked up and Erick was giving me stone eyes. I slipped my phone into my purse. "Oh yeah, the lawn guy didn't show up and after that rain last week, the yard is a forest."

"Did you call?" he asked.

"No, can you do it tomorrow?" I didn't mind handling most of the household business, but it was nice when he was home to do it.

"I don't see why he wouldn't show up."

A server placed my salad in front of me and, in front of him, a hot roast beef panini. I took my phone out of my purse, ready to snap a pic.

"Dammit, Iris."

"Ooo, Daddy said a bad word." Jersey covered her small mouth.

"I'm under contract *and* people are genuinely interested in what I'm doing throughout the day," I said matter of fact. I got why he was annoyed. He was a private person, and not to mention, a few generations behind me so Instagram and Twitter were things he had no real concept of.

***

I met Erick under strange circumstances. We were both trying to catch a flight at LAX. He was on his way home to Dallas and I was making a connecting flight, headed to Hawaii when a man collapsed in front of me in the security check line. I was tempted to back away and call for help but everything happened so quickly. Before I knew it, Erick was down on all fours in front of me reviving the guy and talking to me, assuming that I was the man's companion. There was no time for an explanation and I started helping him. Well, I was helping until the guy started foaming at the mouth. As disgusted as I was by the whole scene, I was impressed the way Erick jumped right in and kept working even after things got gross. And just before the EMTs arrived, the man started coming around and regaining his color. I couldn't believe what I'd witnessed. He was a hero. A real one.

When the whole scene was under control and over, we both discovered we'd missed our flights. We had a couple of hours until the next ones were available, so we sat at a bar getting acquainted. After two pink martinis, which was two too many for me, I became really familiar.

"So, I notice you're not wearing a wedding ring." This was two martinis in.

"No, I'm not." He sipped on black label rum and was on his third.

"I'm smart enough to know that means very little so, are you married?"

"I'm married to my work."

Relieved, I shifted in my seat, hiking up my skirt a little. I knew he was considerably older, but I didn't care. I had a weakness for a man who could make things happen and I had just witnessed him saving someone's life. It got no better than that.

"What do you do, Iris?"

"Travel agent and I do some modeling and acting. I'm thinking about opening a bookstore... or a dress shop. I don't know... I do a lot of things, actually."

"Sounds like it." He sipped more from his glass.

"I know what you're thinking." I placed my drink on the bar counter, waiting on his judgment.

"I'm not thinking anything. You're young so you should be exploring all avenues." He placed his warm hand on my bare knee. "Relax. You're doing what people your age should be doing; trying out many things to find their true interests before settling into a career they'll soon grow to hate." He squeezed my knee and withdrew it upward, dragging his finger toward my inner thigh.

Between the drink, his eyes, and warm hands, I was wet. We made eye contact and held each other's gazes for the longest time. If he had tried even a little, I would've given it up right there in an airport broom closet. But he was a gentleman until the end, later confessing that he knew he could've had me out of my panties, but he didn't want me to regret it. And he wanted to see me again, so he kept his cool.

"Are you vacationing in Honolulu?" he asked breaking the trance we both seemed to be in.

"I'm meeting my boyfriend."

"Oh, I see," he said unfazed. "I would really like to keep in touch with you."

I finished off the last drops of my martini and said, "Do you think that's a good idea?"

The good doctor produced a card from the inside pocket of his sports coat and placed it on my lap, touching my leg once again. "It's your call. When you get home from your vacation with your boyfriend, get in touch with me." He stood and looked at his watch.

I let the card sit at the hem of my skirt, simply glancing down at it. It was just his name, Erick Hart M.D., and a phone number. I could hardly wait to log into Google.

Erick motioned for the bartender to close the tab. "You still have another hour, are you sure you don't want a sandwich or something?" He didn't wait for me to answer. "Hey, add a sandwich for the lady and close me out." He turned to me. "I want you to be able to make your flight this time."

All of the sexual tension in the air left us silent and staring at each other. I could hardly stand it, so I kept counting from one to ten in my head, over and over.

Erick signed the bill and tucked his credit card away. "By the way, where do you call home?"

"Arkansas. Little Rock." I slipped his card into my purse.

"Well Iris, thank you for keeping me company while I waited on my flight."

"Thank *you*." I wanted to say so much more but only inappropriate things swirled around in my head, so I didn't trust what might fall out of my mouth.

"And I *really* hope to hear from you."

With that, the back of his hand brushed up against that same thigh of mine and he backed up and faded into a crowd.

Three months later what's-his-name and I had broken up and I called Erick. A month later he flew me to New York to meet him and a year later we were married. And with every passing day, despite our differences, I loved him more and more.

"Iris, we already get to spend so little time together. Can you just respect that and lay off when I'm here?" Jersey was feeding him French fries from her plate.

"You're right, baby." I tossed my phone in and snapped my purse closed. "Sorry."

Erick blew me a kiss across the table and all was, again, right with the world.

Three

Amy Hart

...the best years of our lives...

The results were slowly coming together. I turned this way, and that. Standing in front of the mirror covering an entire wall in our master bathroom, I twisted and posed. Butt was plump, and stomach was still flat from last year's surgeries and there was only one bandage remaining, waiting to be removed from my nose of this year's face work. Yeah, black don't crack but I didn't get enough of it when I was being made, obviously. So, I had no problem letting a doctor do what God hadn't.

The very thing I used to enjoy, I came to no longer stand. And it only took me fifty-five years to get there. Blending in with white people became intolerable. When I was young I chose when, in a diabolical way, to use my pale skin and blonde hair. There were only a few times when I figuratively checked the Caucasian box but most of the time it was assumed and checked for me with little to know protesting from me. I was ashamed to admit it, but it was my truth.

It wasn't that I didn't like Ws, or that side of myself, after all, that would be self-hate, but what I didn't like was how *they* just didn't get it. And I really wanted them to get it. So, the more life experience I had, the more *they* were on my nerves for not getting it. I also wanted my brother to get it.

Alan took after family on our father's side. Because my father was a fair skinned black man and our mother being white, it was odd that Alan's beautiful complexion was more than a little brown. It was a complexion I loved and envied and one he despised. He resented that the rest of us were 'white' as he put it. His issues with color kept us from having a real brother-sister relationship and once he graduated high school, he basically went out into the world, severing contact with all of us. It broke my mother's heart, ultimately attributing to her early death. I'd lost my brother, my mother, and when my father's health was failing, Ricky was there to help me put my life back together.

Ricky wasn't my first black boyfriend, but he was the first one that my father placed his stamp of approval on. But the last few years of his life, he seemed to not have much to say to or about Ricky. He never said why, he'd just go quiet whenever Ricky was around. I blamed it on his failing health which was on a steady decline the last few years of his life. The day before cancer won the war on his lungs and brain, he told me to take care of myself and to make sure I had money in an account with only my name on it. I lumped that in with all of the other irrational things the brain cancer was causing him to say.

It was heartbreaking for Ricky to watch my father turn on him because he had adored Ricky in the beginning—when we were both brand new to adulthood. Even after my father had been gone for a decade Ricky wouldn't talk about what ever happened between them.

My freshmen year at Howard was when we met. Ricky was a senior and we were at a campus party, partying hard. I had totally embraced black college life—the unique educational process as well as the social side. I didn't know it at the time but those were some of the best years of our lives—individually and as a couple.

For the first decade of our marriage we kept in close contact with college friends and that helped us stay together. Once we moved to Texas we were isolated from our foundation and slowly became like roommates. We got along great and our intimacy was more than satisfactory, but there was no regular romance. Dinner and flowers on anniversaries, fine jewelry and sometimes a car on birthdays or Christmas was expected and given.

At first I wanted the hot passion more than anything else. I wanted the declarations of undying love and to be the thing that Ricky couldn't live without the way it was. But I learned that the only thing he couldn't live without were his patients. They, separately and collectively, were the loves of his life. Without them, he would have no reason to exist; no reason to go on. So, I did what any other homemaker would do in this situation; I focused on our children and tried to find my own way.

Whenever I'd get that lonely feeling, I'd remind myself how good Ricky was to the children and me. And all I had to do was compare my complaints to other women I knew, and I would come to the conclusion that I had no real complaints. Yes, he worked 24/7. Yes, the excitement of our sex was a series of hits and misses. Yes, I knew he placed his patients over his family at times. But he wasn't gambling our money away. He wasn't an alcoholic or drug addict. Now, I didn't think he was a saint and I knew women had been after him for years, but I had no reason to think he'd been unfaithful in any meaningful way. Did I think I was the only woman he'd been intimate with in the 27 years of our marriage? Hell no. I had firsthand proof that wasn't the case. But, I was his wife at the end of the day, whatever he had done, or not done, was of no real consequence to me. He took care of home and he took care of me.

We had only been married a few years when I learned Ricky loved women. I suspected but didn't know for sure until one day that suspicion was founded. That first time I didn't think I'd ever get over it. But I did. So, the next time it was different. No panic, no incredible disbelief, no paralyzing shock, no thoughts of murder.

***

There had been a big sale at Nordstrom and I had done my damage, stumbling through the back door of our home, weighed down with packages. I hadn't heard anything and didn't even notice the pair of red Payless pumps next to the sofa. I had dropped everything in the hallway and rushed to the powder room just off the garage.

I relieved myself but before I could flush, I heard a woman's voice. I pulled my panties and skirt up and quietly stepped back into the hallway. When I heard voices coming from upstairs, I made my way up there. No one should've been home, but I thought maybe one of the kids had come home with a friend. I actually couldn't imagine a scenario and certainly never expected to see Ricky since we'd already been through this. *He wouldn't do this to me again. Surely.*

I moved at a normal pace up the stairs. When I realized the voices were coming from our master suite, beads of sweat formed on my forehead and in my armpits. I stood outside the closed double doors and listened to moans and groans and the sounds of sheets rustling. I sucked in a deep breath and held it. I didn't make a conscious decision but the next thing I knew, I was standing in the doorway watching some wide-hipped, busty redhead straddle Ricky.

I stood unnoticed in the doorway for several moments. I didn't take in the details of what was happening at first, maybe it was too much listening to her talking dirty and watching her hips gyrate over him. At some point I ended up standing next to the bed, just over them. Ricky's eyes were closed, the name Abigail was tattooed on the woman's hip, and dank perspiration hung heavily in the air. Those were the things I noticed. The things I remembered.

When Ricky finally opened his eyes, noticing me, I remained calm. Then, we made eye contact, with his eyes reading panic, and mine, void of emotion. Even I was surprised at my demeanor and I was certain he was too.

The woman turned her head, obviously trying to see what had ghosted him. "Dr. Hart," she said sharply and snatched the sheet covering her front.

"Dr. Hart," I echoed her, realizing at that moment she was most likely someone from the hospital.

"Amy..."

"Hi, I'm Amy—as he just said." I gave a slight wave to the woman just before she slowly turned back to Ricky.

"Um... Glenda," she introduced herself.

"Not Abigail?" I pointed to the tattoo.

The woman followed my finger as if she hadn't remembered what was there.

Before she could respond, Ricky slid her off him and swung his feet over the edge of the bed, reaching for his crumpled boxers on the floor.

"Sorry to interrupt your fucking session on my new sheets," I directed towards him as he rushed by me in search of his slacks.

By this time Glenda was hurriedly searching for her things. "What's going on?"

"You were in bed with my husband."

Glenda had slipped into her panties and her khaki-colored dress, but she was holding her bra. Her eyes moved back and forth between Ricky and me. "Hey, look..."

"Don't worry about it. This isn't the first time and right now, I'm more pissed about my sheets."

"Amy—"

"I'll deal with you later," I interrupted him. "Get her out of here." I still wasn't angry and even I knew that wasn't normal. But, I had been there and done that. What would be the point in going through the drama again?

Ricky had confusion all over his face and for some reason I enjoyed that. He was so smart about most everything and I loved it when he didn't understand something.

To cut across the field, Ricky moved out for six months but eventually we made our way past that rough patch—once I decided to accept that my husband was a womanizing whoremonger. Okay, that's a little harsh. The truth was, Ricky craved constant attention from women. That attention ultimately turned into sex. And that's the truth. He slowed down over the years and that was only thanks to the pure adoration he received from his patients.

Once I understood that about him, it was easy to remember why I loved him. He was my friend—he was my family. We had been a part of each other's lives for so long, I didn't know how to be without him and he made no mention of leaving me for good. I asked him to stop bringing his whores to my house and as far as I know, it never happened again. Intimacy was on life support between us, but we remained married friends. It wasn't just for the kids, either. It was just the easiest thing for us to do.

***

I slid into my new linen pantsuit. It was a shade of pale blue that matched my eyes perfectly. I was planning to rush off to my doctor's appointment, anxious to see the full and final results of my new face, hoping to look great for an afternoon meet-up with Coach Wagner. But that plan slowly fell apart when I heard the garage door coming up. I grabbed my handbag lying in the chair and headed down the stairs, through the kitchen, and towards the back door. I wanted Ricky to see me headed out before he started a conversation.

Ricky mostly slept at the hospital days at a time, so I never really knew when he'd be coming home. And with the kids both away at college, I increased my hours at the dance studio, so I was rarely home during the day. We never knew when we'd actually lay eyes on each other and I stopped complaining about it years ago.

"Hey..." Ricky came through the door quietly, peeling off his scrubs. "Where are you off to?"

"You know what day it is." The plastic surgery I'd had was no secret even though I had been tucked away in the house for weeks with bandages practically from head to toe.

"That's right; today's the big reveal."

I clicked my tongue and winked even though I knew he wasn't even looking my way.

Just before stepping into the laundry room, Ricky stopped and turned around. "How about lunch to celebrate the new you?"

Ricky hadn't joined me for a meal outside the house in so long, I could hardly believe he was asking but I guess he wanted to be first to see what he had paid for. "What, today?"

"Well, yeah... I could even join you at your doctor appointment."

At first I didn't know how to respond but then I figured he wouldn't question me, so I said, "I already have lunch plans." I didn't know what I would say if he inquired with whom those plans were. But he didn't.

"Change 'em." Ricky was down to his underwear, holding his scrubs, headed to the shower. "You should show off the new you. Let's go out— spend the day together."

"Okay, I guess." I sat my purse on the kitchen counter. "How quickly can you shower and dress?"

"Ten minutes." He dashed up the back stairs and seconds later I heard shower water.

I dug my phone out of the bottom of my purse.

```
Hey... so sorry...
something suddenly
came up.
```

I typed, feeling like Marsha Brady—less the text messaging.

```
I have to cancel
lunch.
Dinner instead?
```

I then silenced my phone and waited on an answer. Unlike Coach Wagner, I frequently cancelled one of our meetings, so I was sure he wouldn't be surprised. I really wanted to keep our date, but I didn't know how to get out of Ricky's proposal to spend the day together. I just hoped Coach wouldn't be too angry since I'd refused to see him while I was healing.

```
Dinner will be fine.
What time?
```

I didn't have an answer, but I would let him know as soon as I did.

***

After chumming it up with the plastic surgeon, his med school buddy, glorifying his work, Ricky drove me to the salon and sat in the waiting area while I received highlights and a haircut. It felt a little like old times, so I tried not to overthink it.

The complete new me sat across from Ricky on the patio of a cute little place he chose for what turned out to be a late lunch. I was looking and feeling like *People* Magazine's Most Beautiful Woman with my face wrinkle free and my newly cut hair slightly blowing in the breeze. I hadn't felt that way in a long time, like my old self—or rather, my younger self. We enjoyed cocktails and grilled fish, having conversation that was both strange and familiar. I constantly caught my reflection in the window's glass next to us and I was more than happy with what I imagined would be Ricky's view of my new face.

"Can you stop looking at yourself for one minute?" he asked jokingly over an icy platter of half-eaten oysters.

"I can't help it," I said, blushing, not really embarrassed that he'd caught me, but because I was surprised at how great the day was going.

"You do look beautiful—I mean, you always have—" Ricky leaned in, reaching across the table, and touched my hand.

"What's gotten into you today?"

"This is long overdue."

"I don't want to start an argument but what, exactly, is long overdue?"

"Look, we've been together half of our lives, built a life, raised two children together—we aren't enemies…" He squeezed my hand. "…and we still love each other—if I'm not speaking out of turn."

I tossed my hair over my shoulder with one hand and took ahold of his hand that had been covering mine. I sucked in a deep breath and whispered, "As long as I live, I'll love you." I let go of his hand and picked up my margarita, taking a sip. "I don't know if you deserve it, but it's a fact."

"I assure you, I don't. But, that's precisely the reason *I love you*. After everything we've been through—"

I wanted to remind him of the years of neglect and cheating but what good would that do? Plus, I was enjoying this—all of it—and didn't want the tide to turn with harsh reminders of all the rough patches in our past. I wanted to stay focused on what was happening in the moment—what I was feeling and seeing. Like Ricky's slender frame that was dressed in a gray and white pinstriped suit with a white open collar shirt, bathed in one of my favorite colognes. As men go, he aged incredibly well—hence my need to try and keep up.

"—I know I could've been a better husband to you, and a better father to Korey and Kiley. But…

34

we can't go back, only forward." He took a long swig of his Dos Equis, picked up an oyster shell and sprinkled hot sauce over it. "Instead of rebuilding what we had, let's work at building something new. We don't want the old relationship. We want something new, right?" He slurped the delicacy while watching me.

"I've been seeing someone," I blurted out. "I mean—I've been talking to someone. It hasn't gotten serious or anything, but..."

"I assumed as much and I don't mind admitting that I'm happy it's not serious."

The waiter placed baked, parmesan crusted halibut in front of me and pan-roasted swordfish with peppercorn butter in front of Ricky. We said grace and dug in.

"So... is that who you had plans with today? You know this morning, you said you already had plans."

I didn't answer; I just smiled. "Oh, my God. This is so good!" I forked up a nice sized piece of the halibut, placing it on his plate. "You have to try this."

Ricky laughed a little, tasted the treat I'd given him, and nodded his approval. "That's delicious."

I promptly reached across the table, getting a fork full of his swordfish and stuffed it in my mouth.

"You like it?" he asked me.

"Hmm... not as much as I like mine," I said with a full mouth.

The banter remained light and easy the rest of the day. It was clear that we were both trying hard not bring up anything that would crush the mood. We laughed, we joked, and conveniently forgot about the past. It felt like love.

By the time we reached the house, the sun was setting. We opened a bottle of Riesling, Ricky turned on music, and we slow danced in front of the picture window in our living room. We kissed and held each other before making our way up the stairs.

Wine was still being poured when we found our way under the duvet. Ricky covered my neck, shoulder, and back with kisses and I covered his face and lips the same way. Our legs were entangled under the sheets and 'I love you' dripped from our tongues.

The love we made was incredible and better than I remembered. I didn't know what had gotten into him and I didn't have the energy to ask. I also knew there was a chance that things would most likely go back to the same ol' same ol'. But I made a decision to just enjoy the moment.

"I can't wait to grow old with you," Ricky said, breathing heavily and resting back on his pillow.

"Isn't that what we're already doing?"

"You know what I mean — dentures, canes, walkers." He laughed a little.

"Any dentures, cane, or walker will all be yours, so speak for yourself."

Ricky laughed louder this time, rolled over, and reached for his pants on the floor. When he dug his phone from a pocket, the excitement dimmed inside me.

"You expected at the hospital tonight?"

"Not until the morning."

"And then the fairytale ends..."

"Every day can't be like today, but I promise, things will be better between us." He kissed my lips once more and whispered, "I promise."

Four

Rose

...everything looks good here...

If I'm being honest with myself, I've had the ability to sense when things were about to fall apart since I was a kid. I may not have known in what way they were falling apart but I would stand guard and sure enough, all hell would break loose. I had that feeling when we returned from Cozumel and it became stronger with every passing day.

"Good morning, Mrs. Freeman. How did you sleep?" I was making rounds, checking on patients. Irene Freeman was the third stop with two more to go.

"Better than the night before."

"That's good to hear." I pulled open her blinds, letting the sunlight in.

"Thanks for giving in on the pill." Mrs. Freeman wasn't a hypochondriac more than an exaggerator of symptoms. I had successfully implanted a pace-maker to correct her arrhythmia six months earlier, but every little thing had her running back to see me. And my holistic approach to medicine went against her longtime habits of pill popping so I'd never figured out why she remained one of my loyal patients.

"Yeah, you wore me down last night," I said, giving her an insincere laugh. "Don't expect that to happen tonight. Today, only decaffeinated drinks." I made the change on her diet chart and slipped it on the clipboard. "That'll help you fall asleep naturally."

Mrs. Freeman grunted.

I knew what that meant; she didn't like giving up caffeine. She didn't like most things I suggested. And she certainly didn't like me discussing her health, or as she called it, her "personal business" in front of her roommate so I made it a point to either whisper or write things down for her to read. But today I waited until she was alone while her roommate was out getting a CT scan.

I checked over the readout for her heart's rhythm, checked her IV fluids and other vitals. She was doing great and probably didn't need a stay in the hospital, but I knew it would put her mind at ease. I seemed to only have either risk-taking patients or overly cautious patients and she's definitely one of the cautious ones — which, I'll admit, a brush with death would make most people keenly concerned.

"I'm going to monitor you for one more day, but I expect you'll be ready to go home tomorrow."

"Tomorrow?"

"And we're going to try something new. It's a drug." I hated to admit it, but I needed to try something she'd have more confidence in, therefore decreasing her anxiety while increasing her chances of success with the pacemaker. "I think for you, instead of the acupuncture and other remedies I prescribed before, we'll try Rythmol."

Mrs. Freeman's eyes lit up. "Really?"

"Yes, we'll give it a try and see how you do with it. I'll start you on it today and determine a regimen for you when you leave."

There was a faint knock on the door just before it opened. A nurse and an aid were wheeling in Ms. Gomez.

I turned back to Mrs. Freeman and asked, "So, how does that sound to you?"

"Good — good. That sounds real good," she whispered.

"Okay, take it easy today and let your nurse know if you need anything." I turned and made my way to the sink to wash up. "Good timing, Ms. Gomez. I'm filling in for Dr. Hart. He's in surgery all day."

The nurse secured the younger woman of the two patients' bed, and her IV pole, while I dried my hands.

Ms. Gomez was at full attention and didn't appear too happy at my announcement. "Oh, he's not coming by?"

"I'm sorry, he won't make it today, but he gave me specific instructions," I lied a little.

"Well, I can just wait on him..." The overweight woman's eyes moved over me from head to toe. "...if you don't mind."

"Dr. Hart won't be able to check on you until tomorrow." I approached her bed, about to pick up her chart.

"No! Dr. Hart is my doctor and that's who I want looking in on me."

This wasn't the first time something like this had happened. Rick's patients loved him like groupies love Jay Z. I never took it personal because I had my own groupies.

Mrs. Freeman sat straight up in her bed and snatched back the curtain. "Dr. McDaniel is just as good as Dr. Hart—besides, she's his wife so she knows everything he knows."

I politely took ahold of the curtain, prying the thin fabric from her fingers. "It's okay… sit back, relax, and let me handle this." I made eye contact with my patient, letting her know I was capable.

Mrs. Freeman grunted again when I pulled the curtain back in place.

"Ms. Gomez, I'll take note and report to Dr. Hart—"

"Wife?"

"—if there is anything to be concerned with today. He'll be back on his rounds tomorrow."

"I met Dr. Hart's wife a few years ago, so…"

I smiled as politely as I could. This wasn't a first time for this either. "Yes, I'm his wife."

"No—no. I've met Mrs. Hart."

"You met his first wife—I'm sure it was years back."

"It wasn't that many years back," she mumbled slowly, continuing to look me over.

"In any case…" I picked up her chart. "…I will take a look at your vitals, see how you were last night, and report back to Dr. Hart. He'll be happy to know that everything looks good here." I scrolled through the readout from the monitor. "How did your CT scan go?"

"Fine…" She was obviously still unsure about me and who I was to Rick. "How long have you and Dr. Hart been married?"

I smiled and exhaled slowly. "We just celebrated eleven years."

40

"Eleven years?" she asked as if she didn't believe me. "Do you have a little girl?"

"No... I will let him know you're improving and depending on the results of your scan, he may release you by the end of the week. How's that?"

"Dr. Hart has a little girl..."

"Dr. McDaniel," Mrs. Freeman interrupted, pulling the curtain back again. "Can you tell the nurse it's okay if I get an extra dessert? It's for Mr. Freeman when he comes."

As if she had wished him up, Mr. Freeman opened the door while knocking on it with his cane. I pulled the curtain, enclosing Ms. Gomez and myself.

"I'll see what I can do, Mrs. Freeman. Good morning, Mr. Freeman," I called out beyond the barrier.

"G'morning, Doc," his heavy voice echoed throughout the room. Soon after, a kiss was heard that he'd given his wife, and then a few whispers.

"So, Dr. Hart will be by tomorrow, okay?"

Ms. Gomez only stared at me.

"Is there anything else I can do for you?"

Ms. Gomez only shook her head, so I touched her hand, patting it lightly, and made my way toward the door. She questioned me being Rick's wife and at first, I thought nothing of it. As the day moved forward, her questions and the expression on her face kept popping into my mind.

Five

Iris

Virtual hearts floated abundantly...

Erick was home the week I went into labor. The Braxton Hicks contractions had started so he didn't want me to be alone if actual labor kicked in. Even though I was scheduled for a C-section, it was a good thing because it was Thursday at four in the morning and the time had come—and I had promised my followers I'd go live so I touched the Facebook icon, tossed my curls about, and put on a bit of lip gloss while I waited on the page to load.

I had already sent a text to Marigold, my assistant, to come on over or meet us at the hospital. Jersey was tucked away in bed and Erick was down the hall knocking on the guest bedroom door where my mother was.

I tapped the "live" button and cleared my throat.

```
"Who's up? Anybody? I
know it's four in the
morning… Oh, there's
Debbie and Sophie.
Hey, Marsha. I was
hoping I wasn't the
```

only one up at this
hour."

Hearts and thumbs-up icons floated across my screen.

Marsha: Is it time???
Sophie: U headed to
the hospital, girl…

More hearts floated onto the screen as other viewers joined in the broadcast.

"Yes Sophie, hubby is
pulling the car
around now.
Contractions are
eight minutes apart
so little Darius is
on his way. Bags are
packed, Range Rover
is gassed up, and I'm
on my way to conclude
this pregnancy
journey. Hallelujah!"

The front door opened and Erick stepped in to grab my suitcase, picked up my coat, holding it out towards me. "Let's hit it."

Marigold stumbled through the opened door, bumping into Erick. "Where's your wife?"

"Hey, Mari." Erick pointed in my direction. "Turn that off, Iris."

"You guys heard that,
didn't you? Hubby is
ready but I'll be
checking back in as
soon as I can…"

Virtual hearts floated abundantly across the screen, filling my real heart with the love of my fans and followers.

Joan: I'm praying for
you!

```
Christopher: go drop
that load LOL
Jennifer: Your baby
is going to be so
cute!
Chi Chi: I'm so happy
for you! Be blessed.
Delia: Prayers going
up... love you,
@BloggerQueen!
Joni: We love you,
Iris!
```

I wobbled over to Erick with the live feed still going and slipped my arms into my coat and stepped into my Uggs.

"Turn that damn thing off," Erick's words squeezed through tight lips.

I sucked my teeth in his direction, painted on a smile, and handed the phone to Marigold as she held it up to my face.

```
"Okay guys, hubby is
ready to go but I'll
go live again after
Darius arrives later
today. Thanks for all
your prayers—love you
all!"
```

Hearts and thumbs-up icons pranced across the screen just as a solid contraction hit me. I signaled for Marigold to sign off, ending the live feed, and grabbed my swollen belly.

"Okay, we'd better go."

"That's what I've been saying." Erick held the door open and waited on us to step towards him. "Mari, please see to it that she does not get back on that device later."

Marigold nodded but she knew who signed her checks.

I realized that Erick was not about the social media life, so I didn't waste energy arguing with him. If I didn't show my face later, my followers would worry that something had gone wrong with the baby or me. And I couldn't have that.

The last time I neglected to keep them posted on my well-being, all kind of rumors and lies were spread and those lies resulted in me having an online war with some low-life woman who posted that I had lost my biggest endorsement and was homeless because I had been sued by the cosmetic company. Instead of ignoring her, I engaged, and then started a back and forth, letting her know I had a successful and loving husband who was a doctor and being homeless was the last thing I was overly concerned about.

My tweet was shared tens of thousands of times and it was even made into a meme and a GIF with my picture, captioned: "Bitch, you don't know me" with an image of me scowling from an older post where I was trying sushi for the first time. It's one of Black Twitter's favorites to use in any given situation. In any event, I got her told and shut her up.

I wasn't interested in the effort it took to come back from ghosting my followers and wasn't interested in arguing with Erick. So, I let him think my silence was compliance. I didn't have the energy to deal with him as well as the contractions.

"Erick, call me once you guys get settled in, okay?" my mother's groggy voice came from down the hall before she appeared in her robe. Instead of tying the belt, she held it closed within her clinched fist. She hugged me, kissed my cheek, mumbled an intense and quick prayer, finally saying, "Amen... take care, sweetheart."

"Amen." I kissed her back as I felt the contraction subside. "Thanks, Mom. We'll call you soon."

I wobbled to the passenger side of the truck waiting in our circle drive and climbed in. Erick closed my door, made his way to the driver's side, and drove us to Ennis Regional Medical Center.

***

It was going on noon when Erick stood over me holding our little bundle of joy all swaddled in blue. I watched him kiss Darius' small head just before placing him back in the basinet.

"How are you feeling, sweetheart?" He turned back to me.

"Pain medication is making things bearable." I shifted in bed slightly. "Is he asleep?"

"Snoring, actually."

"We know who he got that from, don't we?"

Erick sat on the edge of the bed, leaned forward, and kissed my lips. "I have a couple of patients here I'm going to check in on the next building and I have a surgery scheduled this afternoon."

"Today? Can't you postpone it?"

"I would if I could, but this patient can't wait."

I was tempted to pout but I knew the deal. Having the baby today was unexpected so I couldn't really blame him for having to do what he would be doing anyway.

"Don't look like that, sweetie." With the tip of his finger he touched my bottom lip, which was obviously poked out.

"I know. Put on your Super Doctor cape and go save the world. It doesn't mean I have to like it." I exhaled and tried to smile.

"So, doctors wear capes now?"

"You know what I mean."

47

"I spoke to your mother and she'll be here this afternoon with Jersey. Okay?"

"Marigold is on her way back, too." Erick was cool with Marigold, but he knew that her coming back to the hospital meant we'd be working in some capacity.

"Can't you take time off?" he had the nerve to ask *me* that.

"She's coming so I *can* take time off."

He stood, touched my hand, and said, "I'll be back late, once I'm out of surgery, but I'll let the staff know where I'll be if you need me."

"I love you."

"Love you, too, sweetheart." He glanced over at Darius. "We make beautiful babies," he said just before he opened the door.

Six

Amy

...but it was moments like this...

$\mathcal{S}$unlight slipped between the seams of the shades covering the bedroom windows. My head felt as if it weighed a thousand tons and I hoped, as it rested in the crook of his shoulder, it didn't feel that way to him. The position of the light coming through from outside told me it was early, but I wanted to know exactly what time it was. It took all my strength to change positions and lift myself so I could see for sure.

I made it onto one elbow, slowly turning my head to face the clock on the dresser. Shit. It was going on noon and I had planned to be up and out hours ago.

"Are you okay?"

I was trying not to wake him, but I guess it didn't matter.

"Yeah, a little hung over but I'm fine." I sat up in the bed, swinging my feet over the edge. "I had no idea it was this late," I said through a yawn.

"You need to be somewhere?"

"Don't you?"

"No." His hand grazed my bare back. "I was hoping we could have lunch."

I loved my husband, but it was moments like this, not that there'd been so many, that kept me confused. What was I doing? And why was I here? Ricky loved me, I knew that, but what I also knew was I couldn't trust his ass. The way he disappeared for weeks at a time was no longer tolerable. Even though I could always reach him, and he seemed to always be where he said he was, made for a complicated marriage. There was a time when I was totally okay with it, but being older, I need more. I needed companionship every day.

When we were a young couple, I was less needy. I had the kids, my sorority, volunteer work—I had plenty to do. I didn't feel alone or lonely—besides, I knew what I had signed up for. I was fine with it for many years and it worked for us. Things slowly seemed to change. I wanted us to finally settle in. I needed him home more days than he was gone. Yes, we did what was necessary and attended important events together, but I wanted to simply go to the grocery store with my husband sometimes. I wanted us to work in the yard together—rearrange the closets together. Was it all too much to ask? Yeah, it was sweet the way he offered to go to the doctor with me that day but hell, I'd been so used to doing things like that on my own for so long, it actually felt awkward when he wanted to tag along.

I desired having someone around every day. I never thought I would say that, but there I was saying it. Maybe it was the long-awaited night of passion he and I shared that was now making me long for more—or long for what I thought should've been throughout the years of other women and disappearing acts. I wasn't sure.

I had been waiting on the day he would retire and we'd keep each other company over meals at the kitchen table, and then he would dry the dishes after I washed them. I didn't need that before because I knew the time was coming. Well, I'm ready to start preparing for that time for us to finally have a life together. And if we were not going to have a life together, I wanted to have that life with somebody. The experience of rocking chairs, Medicare, and dentures with someone who has loved and known you for years was what I expected. It was what I believed most people wanted, even if they didn't admit it.

"Not this time." I stepped into my panties, and then secured my bra. My new body gave me the confidence to stand in his view while I dressed.

"I had a great time last night," he said.

"So did I."

"It doesn't have to end now." He sat up.

"Yes, it does." I stepped over to the chair where my clothes had been neatly placed the night before.

"At least have coffee."

"Can I take it to go and start on my walk of shame?"

Coach Wagner's chocolate frame stood from the bed with every one of his muscles rippling in his back. He found his boxer briefs on the floor, and then came to stand in front of me. "No shame here," he said as he stepped into his underwear. "I'm just glad you finally kept a date with me."

The night before started out with the two of us having dinner, sharing a bottle of wine at the restaurant, and then dessert and another bottle once we got to his house. Despite the fact that I couldn't get Ricky off my mind, Coach and I enjoyed the evening, laughing, talking, and even slow dancing in front of his fireplace. It was nice. It was nice enough to make me want to stay the night.

Spending the night was not something I had planned but I enjoyed myself. And once my clothes were off, I didn't even think about leaving. The wine I'd consumed all evening removed the guilt I would've normally felt. My husband was on my mind, but I reminded myself that he wasn't home — so why should I be?

"I know... sorry." I exhaled, ran my fingers through my hair, and turned my head, searching the floors.

"They're at the back door, remember?"

"What?"

"Your shoes."

"Oh — right." I started towards the door. "I guess I better get going."

"Dinner tonight?" He stepped into his slacks from the night before and followed me out of the room.

"Sorry, Coach."

"Amy, when are you going to start calling me David?"

An uncomfortable laugh came from my throat just before I turned to face him. "It's a habit, that's all."

"Now that we've seen each other naked, that habit needs to be broken."

"Agreed."

We made our way down the stairs, through the kitchen, and to the back door, leading to his garage. The roar of the garage door opening filled the silence, making it easy for me to keep moving.

Coach opened my car door, pulled me in closely, and planted a long kiss on my mouth. I wasn't sure of the surroundings outside because it was dark when we'd arrived the night before so that was the only thing on my mind. I broke away from the kiss and immediately looked out and around.

There was an alley and a field lush with bushes and trees, so I exhaled. Next to my silver Mercedes inside his garage was his black Audi and the night before was slowly coming back to me.

"Thanks again for a great time last night." I tossed my purse on the passenger seat.

"You sound like we won't be seeing each other again."

"What do you mean?" I got in my car, leaving the door open.

"Something in your voice." He stepped back and held onto the handle. "I haven't forgotten your situation so, no pressure."

"We'll see each other again," I assured him.

With one hand he touched his bare chest and with the other he closed my car door and stood back. There was a slight smile on his lips as he headed back inside.

I started my car, put it in reverse, and slowly backed out—not really happy to be headed home but certainly feeling a sense of relief.

I hit the Bluetooth on the dashboard and dialed my voicemail. The first two messages were from Kiley asking me to call her back. Those were the "I need money" messages that I'd learned to identify. The third message was the drycleaner explaining they still couldn't get a stain out of a dress I'd sent back. The last one was from a woman with a familiar name that I couldn't place:

> Hello Amy, this is Rose McDaniel—
> Dr. Rose McDaniel. I'm sorry to
> contact you like this as it's been years
> since we've met. If you could call me

back when you have a free moment, I would certainly appreciate it. Thank you so much."

I wasn't sure if the voice was familiar, but the name certainly was. I was, however, sure it was someone I knew through Ricky. But I couldn't imagine why she would be calling or why she wouldn't simply say what she wanted in the message.

Seven

Rose

...my soft place to land.

Women aren't stupid, in general. They are gifted with intuition and their brains were wired to multi-task in amazing ways. And when it comes to wisdom, a woman is equal to any man. A woman's downfall is she craved love in a way that made her do stupid shit. She will overlook things and second-guess her God-given ability to see through the crap others did. Yeah, loving a man can have a woman all fucked up.

Not thinking things through, I made the call. I didn't know what I was going to say so it was a good thing she hadn't answered. In fact, I preferred leaving the message. I wasn't usually impulsive but the urge to hear Amy reveal the mysteries of the man I loved, and the man she used to love, was strong in a way I couldn't ignore; at least in that moment.

I didn't regret making the call, but I was glad to be granted some time to think. And, I needed it. The thoughts that were running through my head were making me panic. And I wasn't a person who panicked. But I *was* a person who liked to be prepared. Not that anyone liked to be surprised with bad news, but I utterly hated it. So, to be prepared, I practiced what I was going to say when Amy called back. Hopefully, after some basic pleasantries, I'd jump right in and ask her: *"How long have you and Rick been divorced?"*

Amy would give me her answer and I'd explain why I asked in the first place. We'd laugh through it, exchange more pleasantries, and everything would be cool. It had been obvious for years that she'd moved on, so to speak. There didn't seem to be any animosity on her side and there certainly wasn't any on mine. Aside from Rick paying some of her bills, she hadn't bothered us at all. Not even when it came to the kids, which would've been totally understandable.

Rick's kids. I'd been around them a few times, but he mostly went to see them. I never liked that he kept them separate but I was never really a kid person and was certainly not in love with the idea of trying to win over moody teenagers. I had once told Kory and Kiley they were welcome to come over for visits whenever they wanted but they just stared at me, not expressing one way or the other on how they felt about the invitation to our home. It was cool. Work was my life, so I was happy to be absolved of that burden. I didn't want children of my own, so I could live with or without his.

As I played out the phone scenarios of Amy and I, I stood in the kitchen with a skillet handle in one hand and a spatula in the other. Eggs, resting in alternative butter, sizzled and fried. Two butter-loving cardiologists wouldn't dare consume real butter in front of each other. We waited to eat it behind each other's backs.

Rick sipped coffee at the breakfast bar and scrolled through his iPad, checking email. I hadn't told him about the call I'd made the day before but wondered what his reaction would be if I had. Surely he wouldn't care but I kept my mouth closed, waiting to see what I was dealing with first. My intuition was seldom wrong, but this time I was praying it was.

"Just the way you like 'em." I slid purple stoneware, holding two eggs over easy, turkey bacon, and a toasted whole wheat English muffin in front of him — everything hot and to his liking.

The color changed in Rick's complexion and he quickly closed the screen on his device.

"Everything okay?" I asked.

"Thank you, sweetheart." He searched the table. "Butter? Or, whatever that stuff is. And a little jam."

"It's already on there — except the jam. Here you go." I slid a half empty jar of Smucker's onto the counter. "More coffee?"

Ricky simply held out his cup.

With our schedules being so crazy, these mornings rarely happened, and I loved it when they did. The doors to the patio were open so the new day's air coursed through this part of the house. It was quiet with the exception of a distant car making its way down the street several blocks away. I could even hear birds chirping.

"You want to sit out here and eat?" I stood on the threshold, holding my cup of hot tea. I rarely ate breakfast, or at least not anything deserving of a plate. A granola bar, a piece of fruit, a sweet pastry is what I ate, if anything at all. I found more satisfaction in eating lunch. Breakfast was his thing.

"Ben had the revised contract sent over by messenger this morning," he announced. "It's sitting on the dining room table — I've already signed."

The two of us had been working on a device for three years and finally got the patent done and was about to sell it to Johnson & Johnson Medical Devices and Company. I wanted to segue into something and work-related items were a good fallback, so I was thankful he'd changed the subject. We could talk cardio and cutting people open all day without ever becoming bored.

"Okay, I'll sign it now." I continued from the dining room, "Did you ever take a look at the information I sent you on that device? We saw it at that conference in Phoenix. Remember?" I flipped through the pages and signed next to each one of Rick's signatures.

"No, which device?"

"Similar to ours but does everything except connects to a cell phone and it doesn't do a thirty second EKG like ours or allow the patient to send the report to the doctor."

"I haven't seen it," he says while again scrolling through his iPad, answering email from his cell phone. "I need to know more about it."

"Hence, my sending the info to you to learn more. We need to seriously consider the competition. See, theirs would cut out the wait between the patient contacting the doctor, the patient coming in or going to the ER — the medical team could find out immediately if atrial fibrillation is detected. It could change everything."

"I'll take a look later..."

"The downside is the patient would need to constantly be connected to the Internet, or something."

"What's wrong with that?" he asked. "I'm not into technology like that but most of our patients are." Beads of sweat were forming on his forehead.

"Really? I can't tell," I injected, attempting to make a joke. "What are you reading?"

It was as if he didn't hear me.

Rick hadn't taken his eyes off his device while continuing to eat so I loudly scooted back a chair, sat my mug down on the black rod-iron patio table, and took a seat. A light breeze kissed my cheeks. "Hey." I blew on my tea and took a sip trying to create noises. "I forgot to tell you..." I turned back to see if I'd finally captured his attention. I hadn't. He was still scrolling and reading, rubbing his chest. "Remember the other day when I looked in on your patients for you?" I was still waiting on him to acknowledge I was speaking to him. "Babe?"

"Hm?"

"You okay?"

"A little indigestion, I guess." He lightly pounded his chest with his fist.

"The other day when I did rounds for you, remember?"

"Yes, what about it." The iPad was placed on the counter, along with his phone, and Rick concentrated on his breakfast.

"Ms. Gomez — that wouldn't let me examine her — with the peripheral artery disease..."

"Yeah."

"She said something strange."

I heard his fork land on the plate, which signaled to me he was done eating. He didn't respond so I assumed he was waiting for me to finish.

"She said she'd met your wife, while accusing me of not being her."

It took him a minute, and then I heard him coming towards me. He stepped out onto the patio, placed his cup of coffee on the table, and pulled back a chair. "Yeah, that *is* strange." He rested in the chair across from me. "Do we have something around here for indigestion?"

I made eye contact with him. "And then she asked if we had a little girl."

Rick put the mug up to his mouth and took a long sip, still holding my gaze. When he placed the mug back onto the table, he let out a slight chuckle, saying, "What?"

I searched his face. Not knowing what I was expecting to see, but if there was going to be something there, I wanted to capture it. There was nothing. "That's what she asked me."

"She's a sweet lady. I don't know why she's confused."

"And then she wanted to know how long we'd been married."

"Well, technically we're not," he scoffed. It was something he frequently held over my head.

"We are according to the state of Texas. Anyway, I just thought it was strange and wanted to tell you about it."

"Bless her heart — literally," he joked.

We both laughed at that a little and I wanted to let it go. I did let it go but only for a minute. It's not that I didn't trust Rick, but our life together was so open and unconventional that my spirit remained on alert. As much as I wanted to rest and ignore, I *stayed* on alert. He wasn't a perfect man and our relationship wasn't perfect, however, it seemed perfect for us. We did mostly everything together. We shared everything it seemed. He was my rock and my cloud. He was and had always been my soft place to land.

"I'd better be getting to the hospital," he said, interrupting my thoughts.

"Yeah, me too." I drank the last bit of my tea. "But first, the kitchen needs cleaning." I stood, picking up both cups.

"I can do that. Get dressed while I clean up and we can leave together and drop off the signed contract." He took the cups from me, kissed my lips, and entered the kitchen.

I hated how I felt. Even though everything was so normal, the alarm in my spirit was disturbingly loud.

***

After changing my plans and sending Rick on ahead to drop off the contract, and then to the hospital, I sat at the desk in our study, not believing what I was finding—or not finding. I never had a reason to check before but there was no official record or documentation of him divorcing Amy. There were all kinds of sites on the Internet where public divorce records would be listed and his and Amy's was nowhere to be found. A search could be done throughout the country, by state, and even by county. I did it all. Most of the sites were free but some charged a fee. I did the free ones and I paid, yet, there was nothing.

None of it made sense. Why would he propose to me if he weren't divorced? Even better, why would he pressure me to get married if he was still married? I knew Rick well—his challenges, his assets, his flaws—I knew him. He was a man that took care of business with his patients but sometimes neglected things at home, leaving them to me. I knew he was proud of his career as a surgeon but worried about what the general public thought of him. I knew he needed to be loved by his patients but was unsure about the love his own children had for him. I knew he loved praise in general, wanting everyone to adore him. But did I know everything that he was capable of?

Rick's attitude of needing to be adored wasn't abnormal in our profession so over the years, I'd overlooked it; but, what now? Amy still hadn't returned my call but in light of the new information, involving her didn't seem like the best thing to do. This really should be between Rick and me. At least for now.

I picked up my keys and phone, headed to the garage. I honestly didn't want to wait a minute more. I felt like a crazy woman, but the sun wouldn't set on another day with this mystery hanging over my head. *Are Rick and Amy still married? Had he been too lazy to get a divorce?* I had questions that I was afraid to get the answers to—and I was afraid to not get the answers to.

The Bluetooth connected in my car and I waited for Rick to pick up.

"Hey sweetie, you on your way in?" was how he answered my call.

"Yeah, I just walked out. Can you meet me in your office? We need to talk."

"This sounds serious. Everything okay?"

"I don't think so. It's about you and Amy—but we'll discuss it when I get there."

"Amy?" He let out a long, loud breath. *"Did we get another one of her bills?"*

"This is much more serious than a bill. I'll be there in a few minutes."

First there was silence, and then he spoke, *"Okay... I'll be in my office when you get here."* His tone was resolving, as if years of exhaustion was about to be put to rest.

"Did you take something for that indigestion?"

"I'm fine. I'll see you when you get here."

"Okay."

"I love you," he spat out, and then disconnected the call.

As fate would have it, just before I pulled into my assigned parking space, my phone rang and 'Amy Hart' popped up on the display.

Should I answer?

Do I send it to voicemail?

I stared at the screen as the ringing continued and until I no longer had to make the decision. Not knowing if I would even need to call her back, I took in a few deep breaths, turned off the ignition, and stepped out of my car.

With every step, I wondered if asking Rick about this at the hospital, our work place, was a good idea. No, it wasn't. But since I didn't seize the opportunity when I had it, who knew when we'd both be home at the same time again. In fact, the hospital felt more like home and home felt more like a vacation spot. At any rate, there was no changing the plan. I had to have an answer today and I was moments away from one.

The corridor was emptier than usual, and I appreciated that because it lessened the chance I would be distracted by someone or some emergency. I passed the window and could see Rick at his desk. A couple of soft knocks on his door and I pushed the handle, opening it slightly.

Rick stared ahead, blankly. I waited on him to acknowledge me, but he kept his eyes straight before him.

I stood in front of him, placed my keys in my pocket and my phone on his desk, and said, "Look, I'm here for straight answers. I'm sure you'll agree that I deserve that."

Rick still hadn't looked my way. And then, I noticed his face was still. "Rick!" I went to him on the other side of the desk, touched his arm, and shook him. His body fell forward while I still held his arm. "Rick!"

He wasn't breathing. I pressed the intercom on his phone and called for a crash cart and lowered him to the floor. It seemed to happen all so quickly because the room was full, and we were all working to start Rick's heart again.

Eight

Iris

...so, I wasn't complaining...

I was too busy to notice that something wasn't right.

Marigold had been blowing up my phone, but I was preoccupied and never called her back.

I was busy—not because I'd been online engaging with my followers, but because baby-duty was non-stop. It wasn't like I hadn't tried to check in with what was going on online, and I knew they were waiting on an update from me, but the minute I tried logging in, I'd get pulled away.

Ghosting for a successful blogger and Internet celebrity was detrimental to that success. If I were missing too long, I could be replaced quickly. Any perfect storm of events could cast a shadow on even the most well-known. Any new trend or even a scandal could shift the focus somewhere else and getting back in front would take a lot of work. Remaining relevant was a daily chore. I had to know current language, all of the hot topics, and, of course, keep up with what was trending—while trying to be what was trending. What and when women buy — or don't buy — a product based on my word and feedback on said product, I have to know what's going on in the world to properly inform and persuade them.

Marigold had stocked several maternity products in my closet waiting for me to try out and post an opinion on. Clothes, shoes, and make up were constantly being sent to me but most recently, nursing bras, post-pregnancy waist shapers, and a ton of baby items, that I'll probably never get through, were waiting for me to try on, open, or unwrap. I did my best not to feel overwhelmed, wondering if I was truly being missed in cyber world.

Darius wasn't sleeping all night but thankfully, Mom was still here helping while Erick worked all manner of hours at the hospital. This was my life and it was no different when Jersey was born, so I wasn't complaining. Not really. I was used to it. Kind of. But there was no mistaking the pandemonium at the house.

Friends and neighbors visited, bringing food and gifts over and all of this, for sure, was helpful. We had people keeping the house clean, so this freed Mom up to help me with the kids. When I was up every few hours throughout the night, she allowed me to sleep during the day when I needed. It was the same routine as before.

Erick was due to come home, taking a few days off from the hospital, but when I'd spoken to him last, he had been delayed. That was nothing new, but I missed him. Holding the baby up to the phone or computer was the next best thing to Erick being home. It helped get me through.

Darius, cradled in the crook of my arm, was nursing while I rocked in a chair in the nursery. There was no sun coming through the window and it sounded as if raindrops were tapping on the window. The baby and I both were being pulled by the Sandman. He'd nurse, and then he'd sleep — nurse, and then sleep. The routine continued as my eyelids got heavier and heavier.

I didn't hear the door open but suddenly Mother was standing in front of me. Her eyes were motionless and there were no creases in her forehead, as it was when she was about to say something. I waited for the crease to form but she simply stood and stared.

"Mom... you okay?" I stopped rocking.

There was still no crease, but her mouth opened.

"Mom," I said much louder.

She swallowed, and a line slowly appeared above her eyebrow. "Erick is working in Dallas — at Baylor, right?"

"What's wrong?"

"On the news..." She pointed toward the door. "Erick..." Her arm was suspended mid-air. "He collapsed — this morning — I think he's..."

"Collapsed?" I unlatched Darius and got on my feet. I placed my baby over my shoulder, lightly patting his back, and twisted my ankle trying to get out of the room.

I heard my mother say, "Let's stop and pray first," as I whizzed by her.

A second later I leaned into the kitchen counter, trying to tune into the television while I opened my iPad. Once it came to life, alerts flooded the screen. I'd already missed whatever my mother had seen on the news, so I figured I could find something online. The alerts were slowing down the operation and then I was curious why there were so many. Sitting in my inbox was message upon message of people sending me a looped video of Erick standing at our front door, taking me to the hospital. The sender asked if Erick and I were married and if I knew he already had a wife. It was an odd thing to ask but, the majority of the messages had a similar tone.

My mother slipped the baby from my arms. "Get to the hospital. I'll be here with the kids." She stepped back. "Glenn is going to drive you."

Glenn was our neighbor and he was waiting in the driveway when I walked out of the back door. His cheeks were flushed but he remained silent while I situated myself in his front seat.

With my purse in one hand and my phone and iPad in the other, I stepped up into his truck while he held the door. My eyes bounced back and forth from both screens as he drove.

Nine

Amy

Tears were rolling down...

It was an hour and twenty-minute trek to Dallas and I probably shouldn't have been making it alone. But the voicemail Dr. McDaniel left me was disturbing, at best. The earlier message she'd left seemed innocent enough but this last one instructed me to get to the hospital as soon as I could.

I had made this drive many times over the years; however, I hadn't made it in a long time. But, not so long that I didn't remember the way. The parking had changed and there were more buildings but there was enough familiarity at Presbyterian Hospital in Dallas for me to get around. The one thing that hadn't changed was the stale smell of disinfectant—the whole reason I hated hospitals. I tried not to breathe in too deeply as I made my way through the maze, reading signs and following arrows.

I rushed down the back hall to Ricky's office where Dr. McDaniel told me to meet her. She was standing outside the door, speaking to another staff member when we made eye contact. We recognized each other's faces.

She ended her conversation, sending the young woman off.

"Hello, Amy." She held out an arm and guided me across the hall through another door. I could see her nameplate next to the door's frame.

I followed her. "Hello, Dr. McDaniel."

She closed the door behind her. "Please, call me Rose." She pointed to a chair in front of her desk.

I accepted her offer and blurted out, "What's going on — where's Ricky?"

"I'm so sorry to break it to you in this way..." She cleared her throat. "But... Rick died suddenly just before I called you." She cleared her throat again and seemed to be struggling to hold back tears. "It appears to be cardiac arrest and I just didn't want to say that over the phone in a message," her voice trailed off.

"Died?" I stood to my feet again. I heard everything she said so I wasn't asking her to repeat herself. "Where is he?"

"I can take you to him but before I do, I just wanted to clear up some things."

"Oh, my God..." My breath was caught in my throat and my chest ached. I watched Rose get me a bottle of water and hand it to me. "He's dead?" I sat again. "Were you there? What happened?"

"Like I said, I think a heart attack. He was in his office... We did all we cou..." her voice cracked as she was losing her battle to hold back tears. "I thought he had been feeling pretty good lately, so this came out of nowhere."

"Well, he was fine when he was home last."

Rose paused a moment and then said, "I wanted to tell you so you could notify his children before they heard it on the news."

"Right." I took out my phone and scrolled through my contacts.

"Here, I'll give you a minute to call and then take you to see him." Rose stepped out and waited in the hallway.

Kylie's name flashed across my screen and that's when I knew I was too late. The Internet moved news at such a speed that bad news made it around the world a hundred times before good news could even get out of bed.

"Kylie. I was just calling you and Kory."

"Is it true? Daddy has another wife?"

"What... no... uh, I was calling... Your dad died today. He had a heart attack."

"What?"

"Let me get Kory on the line. Hold on." I was a pro at conference calling with the kids and I was thankful because the three of us needed to connect.

"Kory? Kylie? You both there?"

"Yes," Kylie answered.

"I'm here."

"Your dad died late this afternoon. I was trying to get a hold of you before you found out some other way." Tears were rolling down my face, but I tried hard not to let my crying come through in my voice.

I heard Kylie crying and I knew my voice would crack if I spoke.

"Where was Dad when it happened?" Kory asked.

"He was in Dallas. In his office at his... They did all they could to save him, so I was told."

"I'm on my way," Kory announced.

"Use your credit card to book a ticket—both of you. Kory, don't try to drive. Just get on the next flight, there's nothing you can do right now. I'm going in to see him so I'll call you both back."

Kylie was openly sobbing so I hated hanging up on her. "Kylie, book a flight and call me back."

"*Mom…*" Kory began.

"You too, Kory. Call me and let me know when you're arriving. I love you bo…" I disconnected the call.

Rose must've heard me end the call because she stepped back in just then. She took her seat behind her desk again, so I followed suit and sat as well. There were tissues on her desk so I helped myself to them once she scooted the box forward.

"Please, know that I hate doing this…" Rose started.

My phone rang, I pulled it out of my pocket, rejected Coach Wagner's call, and put it back.

I made eye contact with her after blowing my nose.

"But, I just don't see a way around it."

"What is it?"

"I had been calling you, as you know, for the past week or so. There was an issue I wanted to bring up with you. Again, please, forgive me for doing this right now but since Rick and I got together eleven years ago, I never thought it necessary to ask him for proof that you and he were divorced and recently — "

"Divorced? Hell no, we're not divorced. What is this about?" I leaned forward.

Rose stared at me for several seconds, swallowed hard, and pushed back from her desk. She remained seated but looked as if she wanted to stand.

Rose cleared her throat. "Rick and I were, for all intents and purposes, m-m-married." She was struggling. "We — we have a home together, we have a business and several research ventures together… a life togeth… He's proposed to me many times but

72

we... for whatever reason, never did. I'm not trying to make this more complicated than it already is, obviously, but he was my husband."

I felt my tears drying and my face warming, surely turning red. "You're delusional. Ricky and I have been married for twenty-eight years and have never *even* been legally separated."

That's when Rose stood to her feet. She turned away from me and for the first time I noticed pictures of her and Ricky on the bookcase behind her.

"That explains a lot..." she said softly.

"Well, explain it to me. What are you talking about?"

"Rick has had two wives all this time and neither of us knew it. There have been signs, which is why I called you. But... I never thought..."

"I want to question what you're saying to me but somehow, for Ricky, it's believable." I suddenly remembered Kylie's question of her dad having a second wife. "So, I guess it's already out there in the news that the good doctor played us for fools. My daughter just asked me."

"Really? I didn't think anyone knew yet. I certainly haven't said anything to anyone else—none of the doctors or staff. And the way gossip flows around here..."

"Look, I don't know what your plan is, but I've been married to Ricky for what feels like all my life. I'm his wife and I'm sorry he lied to you, but I have to protect my children."

Rose and I locked eyes for a long moment. She seemed like a nice enough lady so I imagined she appreciated my position while I sympathized with hers—but not enough to lay down the gauntlet.

"Look, we don't have to figure this all out right now. Let me take you to him." She exhaled and moved to the door.

Ten

Rose

I didn't know how to answer...

$\mathcal{F}$rom the moment Amy opened her mouth, I found myself questioning her ethnicity. And then, I couldn't figure out why I was so focused on that. Pale skin, blond curls, straight nose, and thin lips. What difference did it make? Especially once she made it clear that she and Rick were still married. Had always been married. Had never *even* been legally separated, as she put it, complete with a slight roll of her neck. She was a black woman, clearly. I didn't care that she wasn't white like I had always thought but it gave me something to focus on other than the fact that my husband—common law or whatever—was dead. Rick was dead. He was gone. And now two women had to clean up his mess while working feverishly to keep his reputation untarnished.

I guided Amy to the room where Rick's body lie covered and waiting on someone from the morgue to take it once I gave the go-ahead. I pushed open the door, tempted to walk in with her, but I knew she needed her time just as I'd had mine. I stepped out and paced the hallway wondering how this whole mess was going to work out. What would happen? She seemed fine and agreeable now—her dignity intact—but would that last? I wanted to live in the moment and worry later about the lie Rick had obviously been living.

Being present in the moment took on a whole new meaning when, while I paced the hallway, I heard a commotion coming my way from around the corner. A young statuesque woman who appeared to be in her early thirties followed Dr. Cavazos, Rick's long-time colleague and nemesis. The young woman could easily grace the cover of any magazine even though she was dressed in sweats and a baseball cap covered her long hair—I'm guessing it was weave but I couldn't be sure. Tears were flowing as she whimpered and struggled to breathe.

"Dr. McDaniel, is there somewhere we can go?" Dr. Cavazos asked calmly.

"What's going on? Who is this?"

"There's a situation—trust me, we need privacy."

The young woman stepped closer. "Where is he?" she struggled to get out. Her hand disappeared inside the sleeve of her sweatshirt as she used it to dry her face.

"Who?" I asked her, but wanted an answer from either of them.

"My husband. Dr. Hart." She took in a deep breath. "Did he die?"

I tried gathering my thoughts. What in the world was happening?

"Excuse me?" I managed to say.

"Let's go in your office," Dr. Cavazos kept his tone steady.

The three of us marched off across the hallway with me forgetting I'd left Amy in the room with Rick's lifeless body. We stepped inside and before I could close the door, I spoke up again.

"What's going on here?"

"I was told that my husband — Erick — Dr. Hart, died. Do you know anything or not? I keep getting the run around here."

I didn't know how to answer her, so I added my own question. "Who are you?"

"I'm Iris Hart. Who are you?"

"This is Dr. McDaniel. She's..."

"Look, have a seat and I will be able to give you more information shortly." I turned away from her. Taking her in was too difficult. "Can I speak to you for a moment, Dr. Cavazos?"

"Just give us a moment, please," he said to her and helped her to an empty chair.

"What's going on?" I asked him as soon as the door closed.

"I was hoping you could tell me. She was running around asking questions — got everyone talking all over the hospital. I think there's something going around on the Internet, too. Do you think she's telling the truth?" Dr. Cavazos ran a hand through his wavy cold black hair.

"I wish I could say no. But..." before I could finish, Amy stepped into the hallway, coming toward us. "Let me introduce you to Rick's first wife — and according to her, his *current* wife."

Visibly distraught, Amy wiped tears from her face. She took out her phone ready to make a call. A group of people made their way past us, so I waited until they were around the corner.

"Amy, we've got a new development on our hands."

Dr. Cavazos spoke up, "I'm confused."

"There's another woman here—claiming to be Rick's wife."

"That son of a bitch." Her tears started anew. "Where is she?"

I pointed towards my office. "Let's get this over with."

I opened the door to my office. Iris was staring straight ahead and slowly turned in our direction as I allowed the two to come in after me.

Iris dabbed at the tears on her cheeks and cleared her throat. "So, is he dead or not?"

"Wow, this is crazy," Amy mumbled, clearly not able to wait until proper introductions were made.

"Who are you?" Iris snapped her neck around.

"The question is, who are you?" Amy stepped in closer. "I don't know what kind of game you're running..."

"Look, why don't we all calm down," Dr. Cavazos started.

"And who the hell are you?" Amy was on a roll.

"Hey, this isn't helpful," I said to Amy and then turned back to Iris. "To answer your question, yes, Rick died this afternoon, apparently from a heart attack. We won't know for sure until an autopsy has been done. But first, I'd like to introduce you to Mrs. Amy Hart," I could hear my voice trailing off.

"I don't get it," Iris announced.

"What's not to get? I've been married to Ricky for nearly three decades." Amy's neck was rolling again. "Probably as long as you've been living."

Iris stood to her feet, towering over Amy. "Are you suggesting Erick has another wife—and that wife would be you?"

"No, I'm suggesting that he had two other wives..." Amy nodded towards me.

"Bitch, please."

"Bitch?" Amy stepped in closer, making herself appear even smaller than Iris. "I got your bitch."

Dr. Cavazos stepped between the two women but not before the swearing and profanity flew around the confined space.

I took Iris by the arm, but she snatched away.

"And you too," Iris yelled.

"Hey, Rick—Dr. Hart obviously led secret lives with each of us," I said, noticing the front of Iris's sweatshirt was wet but stopped before pointing to it. I assumed she was nursing but I kept quiet; I just didn't want things to get any more complicated. "Follow me, I'll take you to see him."

Just then, Amy let out a bellowing cry.

We continued out of the door. Amy's heart-wrenching cry started fresh tears for both Iris and me.

"What's happening?" she asked.

"That's what we're all trying to figure out." I stopped in front of the door with Rick's body on the other side and turned to Iris. "Are you nursing?"

Iris looked down at the front of her Texas A&M sweatshirt and cried even harder. She grabbed the bottom of it and fanned it out.

"It's okay, I'll get you some paper towels."

"We have a new baby and a four-year-old." She sniffed and pointed to the door. "Is he in there?"

"Yes." I was glad there was no time for me to consider all that I had learned in the past hour.

"Can you come with me?"

"I think it'd be best if..."

"Please. I've never..."

It was nothing I wouldn't do for any random patient, so I erased from my mind who she was, and the predicament Rick had put us all in and simply opened the door, leading her inside.

I stood next to Rick's young wife with my hand resting on her shoulder as she whimpered over him. What was next? How bad was this really gonna get? How would we, the wives of Dr. Hart, handle the horror of it all? And, who would come out on top?

Eleven

Iris

... tempted to clap back...

There was no escaping the fallout of the trending headline, "Dr. Hart and His Three Wives." It was everywhere. I even heard the story made it to *Entertainment Tonight* with Kevin Frazier reporting. I could only believe that because of my online presence and hundreds of thousands of followers, that there was even any real interest in the story. But, strangely enough, headlines *didn't* read "Online Blogger Finds Out Her Husband Has 2 Other Wives," instead, many of them read, "Renowned Heart Surgeon's Death Unveils 3 Wives." It was all too much.

Erick was dead but time to mourn him would obviously have to come later. Marigold never left my side, sitting on Erick's side of the bed while I pumped breast milk.

"I spoke to your doctor and she's sending over a prescription for sleep, safe enough while you're nursing."

I simply detached the pump, secured my nursing

bra, and turned over in the bed as a response.

"How are you feeling, sweetie?" Marigold patted my foot through the heavy comforter.

"Terrible," I mumbled just before fresh tears burned my eyes.

"Can I offer you some advice?"

"Oh, now you're asking first?" I popped my head up from the pillow.

"Seriously, stop responding to people's comments on Twitter and Facebook. It's not helping the situation."

"The repost of me bragging about having a husband resurfaced. Women are dogging me out big time."

"I know. I saw it — and your response."

I groaned and turned over again.

"You can't do anything about what you tweeted years ago. That's done and over. But, don't get on the level of people who are reveling in the scandal. In fact, don't even read it. Let me keep track of what's going on and I'll let you know when there's something out there that needs to be addressed."

"Easier said than done..."

"Where's your phone?"

I felt Marigold get up from the bed.

"I'm going to uninstall your social media apps — just for a while. I'll keep them up for the time being. I don't want you tempted to clap back the next time a meme is posted."

"There are memes?" My head popped up again.

Marigold stood over me, picking up my phone from the nightstand. "You know people use any situation to make people laugh. Don't worry about it — it'll all blow over in time." She swiped the screen on my phone and typed in the pass code. "But, in the meantime, I'll clear your phone just in case you're curious enough to take a peek."

I buried my head deeper under the comforter hoping for sleep.

"I'll take this milk so your mom can label it and put it in the fridge. I'll be downstairs working and will pick up your prescription when it's ready. Do you need anything?"

I exhaled loudly, which she clearly took as me answering no because I heard the door close a moment later. I patiently waited for sleep to come but until it did, I kept reliving my words from a few years ago—words that, I'm guessing, will live on forever.

The woman, or should I say media troll calling herself TruthBTold, from years ago was back at it with a vengeance. It all started with her lying saying I had lost an endorsement and was being sued by a cosmetic company because another person had an adverse reaction to a makeup product based on my instructions on how to apply it. None of it was true but it took off like wildfire and I felt the need to defend myself. Of course, this woman kept—or found—our exchange from the summer of 2014, reframed my response, making it new and reposted it, and happily refreshed the memories of those who had long forgotten it.

> BloggerQueen:
> Homeless? You're
> confusing me with yo
> family. My HUSBAND is
> a SUCCESSFUL surgeon
> so being homeless is
> nothing I fear even
> if #BeautyTech was
> suing me, which
> they're not. Get your

```
           facts straight! Maybe
           your man is
           struggling to keep a
           roof over your
           head...oh, that's
           right, you don't have
           one. #bitchPLEASE.
```
The ball was rolling then...
```
           TruthBTold: You FAB,
           I don't need to cling
           to a man's success.
           I'm successful within
           my own right!
           #ufakewannabewriter.
           BloggerQueen: A
           success at what?
           Hoeing? FYI, I am a
           world-renowned
           writer, being paid
           BIG $$$ to write
           about products you
           can't afford to buy.
           TruthBTold: Writer???
           :-D :-D Blogging is
           nothing more than
           punctuated graffiti.
           #getoveryourself
```
And that's when it really got ugly. The name calling and cursing each other out bled over onto Twitter, and then it took on a life of its own. Once things died down, the executives at BeautyTech chastised me and I calmed my interactions with the online public down, letting my fans rip that woman apart while praising Erick and I.

As much as I didn't want TruthBTold to have the last word, I didn't have it in me to start that whole thing up again. There were simply too many other things to focus on.

Twelve

Amy

If Ricky wasn't already...

$\mathcal{T}$hree wives and three memorial services—the spectacle seemed to be getting reported on every news show on every channel. Maybe it wasn't, but it seemed to be. Because it was unclear who to release his body to, I couldn't have an actual funeral—and obviously Rose and Iris couldn't either. Within a 24-hour period, there would be three memorial services in three different cities for one man.

Plants and flowers crowded the front of the church, surrounding a large portrait of Ricky resting on an easel. There was a video with a montage of photos of him, the kids, and me. The service was quick and mechanical, no one daring to mention the obvious—the pink elephant in the room. I've never been one to avoid the obvious, so it took all I had not to step to the microphone in the crowded church and be the first to bring it up. I remained seated, imagining myself taking those few steps to the podium and saying how I felt.

"Unless you've been lost in outer space the last few weeks, I'm sure you've seen the news or read online reports." Or, *"Yes, Ricky was married to two other women."* Or, *"No, I didn't know about Ricky's other wives but I'm not as shocked as the rest of you."* Or, *"If Ricky wasn't already dead, I'd shoot the bastard in his cold-blooded heart."* Or even, *"This motherfucker fucked over me for the last time."*

Since I didn't know what to say or how to say it, I remained seated and performed as expected to the end. Since there was no body or casket, it made things easier to get through the service, I think. It was like partial closure—not the finality a funeral and burial offers. I'm not sure if it was good for our children but none of this was good.

We greeted guests and filed out of the church. There were a few reporters posted outside, I'm guessing they were waiting for some drama. I could see a few cameras pointed in our direction but did my best to ignore it, telling the kids to do the same.

After the service, our home was full of family members of Ricky and I: friends, neighbors, as well as other people we knew and loved. A couple of Ricky's aunts and an uncle, a few distant cousins, some of his long-time colleagues—mostly retired doctors—some of my distant relatives, old neighbors, and parents of some of our kids' friends. There was even an old mailman from the first home we lived in and a few of Ricky's earlier patients from years ago. Everyone was supportive of the kids and me, loving us through all of the mess.

My brother arrived unexpectedly the day before. I hadn't seen Alan since our dad's funeral, so I was completely shocked that he was concerned enough about what was going on to come and offer support.

As embarrassing as it all was, I appreciated his presence.

With each person coming through the double doors at our home, I disengaged from my reality and turned into a hostess, thanking him or her for the support. I didn't want any of them to know how totally embarrassed I was for my predicament. Those that truly loved me avoided the news coverage just as I had, and the others fully took it in so they could be ready with their unsolicited advice on how I should handle the other two women. The suggestions ranged from suing them to bringing physical harm. I didn't have the stomach for any of it; however, I appreciated their loyalty towards me.

Alan approached me. I couldn't get over how great he looked—his cocoa-brown skin and slender build made me a little envious of his looks but at the same time, proud. I loved introducing him as my brother. It was visual verification of my blackness—my heritage. Having brown kids didn't even do that because everyone figured they got their color from their dad. But my brother's presence legitimized me as a black woman.

"You look amazing. I know I keep saying it, but you really do," I told him once he put his arm around my shoulder.

"You're looking good too, sis."

"Yeah, thanks to some talented doctors in Frisco."

"If it's okay with you, I'm going to start asking folks to leave," Alan whispered into my ear.

I glanced at the clock. "I think it helps to have them here." I could see Kylie in the dining room in a discussion with her friends.

"We need to talk," Alan announced. "I retained an attorney for you."

"Why'd you do that? I have an attorney."

"You can't use Ricky's attorney. He'll be too cautious, trying not to ruin his friend's reputation. You need someone new."

I exhaled and took a seat at the oversized island in our kitchen. "I don't want to talk about it right now. Mentally, I'm drained."

"That's fine. Get your rest but tomorrow, we're on it."

Insurance papers. Lawyers. Court dates. Court drama. Fighting with Ricky's women. Posturing to claim my position. The mere thought was exhausting. I wanted to go back to—a month ago—a year ago, to my simple life. Back to a time when I was the wife of a doctor that came home when he felt like it and I was more than okay with that. But here I was, neck-deep in Ricky's mess.

Suddenly, I was slicing baked ham, smoked brisket and roast beef. I packed up containers of potato salad, coleslaw and deviled eggs, offering plates of food to the guests in my home. It was my gracious way of saying, "Time to go." Several of my girlfriends joined in and helped me by cleaning the kitchen. Everyone got the hint and left one by one.

Once the house was empty and Alan had gone to bed, the kids and I looked through photos and watched old videos of them when they were small—when Ricky and I were young parents—when we had no idea how good we had it. We reminisced. We laughed. We cried.

Thirteen

Rose

...take your words and twist them.

$\mathcal{I}$ didn't want to live. I didn't want to fight. I didn't want to cry. I didn't want to remember him. I didn't want to remember us. I didn't want to talk about Rick being dead. I wanted to act as if the past eleven years hadn't happened but that was impossible. Each one of our friends and fellow hospital workers needed closure and they were looking for me to provide a way for them to get it.

It was ridiculous, really, all three of us having our own service for the man we claimed as our husband. We were all as different as night and day — as I'm sure our tributes to Rick were. As hard as I tried not to join in the circus of it all, I eventually caved into the pressure and threw something together. I didn't have it in me to put together an elaborate service so there was a carefully worded obituary, a few flowers, and kind words delivered by the Chief Resident.

It was hosted at a newly built recreation center, not far from Dallas Presby, with a small reception following. Dr. Salem Patel spoke softly over a group of a hundred or so doctors, friends, and hospital workers. It was all well and proper. Not too lavish, not too clinical. And it happened so quickly and spur of the moment that the media didn't get wind of it in time to show up. Unlike Amy and Iris, I was spared that particular humiliation.

I tried returning to work. I needed to keep my mind preoccupied, but the situation was difficult to escape. I had friends tell me it would pass and that soon people would turn to the next scandal, forgetting about this one, but I found that hard to believe. It was everywhere.

It was a Thursday, normally the end of my work week but I had been working weekends since Rick died. Sitting home just made me crazy—made me miss him crazy—made me have crazy thoughts. I had taken on many of Rick's patients, so work was plentiful—not to mention our research. My hands were full and I was beyond thankful for that.

"Dr. McDaniel, can you look over an x-ray for me? I'd like your opinion on a patient's case." Dr. Marie Joseph stood in front of me holding CT scans. "Follow me," she added.

I did. Even though I was busy, I couldn't ignore that she grabbed me by the elbow and escorted me off. We ducked into an observation room and she placed the scans on the monitor and flicked the light on.

I studied them closely. "What am I supposed to be looking for?"

I could hear Marie breathing heavily next to me.

"This looks like your basic case of calcium build up in the coronary... am I missing something?" I turned to find her staring at me. "Just a basic by-pass—a double."

"Hey... I wanted to get you alone." She cleared her throat. "I was contacted..." She cleared her throat again.

I waited.

"I was contacted by *Globe* Magazine. They want to pay me to answer questions about you and Dr. Hart."

I took a seat at the table and she joined me.

Marie secured her hair behind her ears. She had been at Dallas Presbyterian for four or five years, a young, single woman dedicated to her career. We'd perform many surgeries together and she had trained exclusively under Rick for the past two years. I could see perspiration forming on her nose.

The heat was rising for me too. "Why are you telling me?"

"I thought you needed to know."

"You know, you're not the first person to come to me with such news."

"No, I didn't know."

"Hey, I can't tell you what to do—I'm sure the money is tempting." I moved to get up from the table.

"Look, I'm *not* tempted. I honestly wanted to inform you that I'd been asked. I have no intention to tell them anything—I don't know anything anyway."

"You know enough, I'm sure."

"The fact is, if I don't talk, they'll find someone who will."

"I'm sure they will, unfortunately," I responded

"I haven't declined yet, but I thought if I did speak to them, I could tell them what you wanted me to. I want to help you. There are so many ugly things being reported that I want to clear it all up." She exhaled slowly. "I've always admired you and

Rick—your personal and professional relationships. I just hate what's happening." I saw a tear well up in the corner of her eye.

"I appreciate the offer, but they can't be trusted. They will take your words and twist them. As much as I believe you want to help, it won't in the end." I touched her hand. "The best support you can give is to remain silent. I am not going to fight for my place as Rick's wife. I just don't have it in me so don't get caught up in this mess. Just remember the man, friend, and colleague he was to you and support me while I make my way through it all."

The tear spilled over onto Marie's cheek and I fought back my own.

"I can do that."

"At some point, it will all die down," I added.

We embraced for a long moment.

"And, in case you can't tell, I truly appreciate you coming to me first. Most everyone has but I'm sure it's just a matter of time before there's someone who can't resist." I gently touched her shoulder. "Again, I appreciate it."

Fourteen

Iris

...flush out all of the ugly...

I had been to three attorneys — all different — and all promising me that I had a winning case against Erick's first wife and that doctor. All I needed to do was choose one of them and be ready to fight. I was ready. I needed a barracuda in the courtroom because I was going for everything that was coming to me for my children. Deciding which one was the most ruthless was where my thoughts remained.

It was tempting to lose focus and get involved in the social media banter, but I kept my mind on what was important — claiming my rightful place as Erick's wife. Besides, people's posts were inflamed on one day and the next there'd be virtual silence. And then, some new development would happen and this whole fiasco would be at the top of everyone's news feed again. And then TruthBTold had a video circulating that'd had a half a million views. Marigold tried to keep me from seeing it, but she was too late.

TruthBTold was reveling in my misery. The thrill

was all over her face when recapping how I bragged about having a husband and painting her as a lonely, bitter bitch. I couldn't let my story end like this. I had to have the last word, which was why I needed an attorney perfect for the job.

My mother joined me each time I met with a lawyer, praying first, and advising me on which to choose. We stepped into the third attorney's office, ready to check her out.

"Hello, I'm Marion Mays," my mother spoke up first, extending her hand.

"Hello, Marion. I'm Greta Baldwin." The plump, blond woman shook my mother's hand while peering past her, looking at me. Her shoes were soft brown leather Crocs, completely broken in, each heel slanting in the opposite direction. Her short hair rested on the collar of her standard white blouse that was tucked inside a navy-blue suit. I could even see dandruff flakes on the shoulders of her double-knit blazer.

"Hello," I spoke up. "I'm Iris Hart."

Greta shook my hand with her right and grabbed my elbow with her left. "It's good to meet you, Iris. Please, both of you have a seat."

My mother and I sat in front of Greta's desk. Her office was huge with stately, heavy furniture with a huge picture window behind her desk. We were in downtown Ennis, Texas so the view wasn't so great. The other highly recommended attorneys we'd visited were located in Dallas and were set up in fancy, contemporary offices. I was almost committed to one of them, ready to cancel my meeting with Greta. Seeing her was making me second-guess my decision to keep the appointment.

I took one glance over at my mother to hopefully read her expression and it was as if she were personally hearing from God. There was a sparkle in her eye that told me she thought we had found who we were looking for. I wasn't so sure just yet.

"So, let's cut to the chase. I normally let a client tell me his or her story and then I decide if I can help them win the case. But due to the notoriety of your situation, I'll tell you what I know and you can fill in what I don't know." She plopped down in her rickety office chair heavily, making it scream for mercy. She slid in closer to her messy desk, pushed her glasses up on her nose, and then folded her hands in front of her. "You're a fashion blogger who married a bigamist and the media is having a field day with it because he's a well-noted heart surgeon. You're not just any fashion blogger but one with enough pull to get Commissioner Williams to show up at your memorial service."

Greta paused as if she thought I would respond but I waited on her to finish.

"And, from what I could tell, you had the biggest crowd at your service between all three, which may indicate that people see you as the legitimate wife. Or, it could just be because you have fame and the media was there, too. You have two small children, in fact you recently gave birth to the doctor's youngest child and that adds another pull on the heartstrings. Of the other two wives, it seems, that he only legally married one of them many years ago so proving that they were no longer married in the practical sense will be our focus. The other woman should be of no consequence since there was no marriage license."

She ran my shit down like it was nothing. Like my life was nothing.

"Okay, so you've watched the news."

"There's no escaping it." She stared at me eye to eye as if she was trying to read my mind. "How is it that Commissioner Williams showed at *your* service?"

"His nephew by marriage has a skin care line, Body Glo, and it's one of the products that I blog about and promote. They make a lot of money based on my articles so I'm sure the whole family felt obligated to show. Money talks."

"That explains it. So, tell me what I don't know."

I exhaled, cleared my throat and began, "We were married for five years—happily. We moved into our home after it was built just shortly after our destination wedding in Cabo San Lucas. He loved our children and was thrilled about our son being born. And... I might add... he loved me."

"Did Dr. Hart reside in the home?" she asked matter of fact.

"Of course."

"You say, of course, but did he have his clothes or personal belongings there? Did he sleep there every night? Receive mail?"

"Yes, his things were there. No, he didn't sleep there every night—he's a doctor. Some nights he stayed at the hospital," my voice went up an octave or two.

"Are you sure that's where he was?"

"Well, I didn't have a GPS on him. He said he was at the hospital and that's what I believed."

"I'm sure you also believed that you were his only wife—or at least his second wife, right?"

"Look, just state your strategy," my mother chimed in. "What's with the degradation?"

Greta turned to my mother. "That's nothing compared to what could happen in court." She turned back to me. "We will need to flush out all of the ugly if we plan to win. And I think you can win."

There was another pause and again I waited.

"First, we will establish what he was worth because if there's nothing to get, there's no need in going through all of this. And then, we'll find out more about the other two women. It won't be an open and closed case but it's one we can win." She exhaled and pushed back, making her chair scream again. "Think things over and if you'd like to retain me, let me know. Ten-thousand up front and I work at four hundred and fifty dollars an hour."

Greta didn't have the look and style I imagined my attorney having but I liked her straightforward attitude. She didn't give a fuck and that's what I needed.

I opened my purse and pulled out my credit card, holding it up in the air.

"Great. See Sammy out front and I'll send you an engagement letter for you to read and sign—let's say, tomorrow." She stood.

"Okay." I also stood, and my mother followed suit.

"Can't wait to get started." Greta stretched out her hand for a final shake.

Fifteen

Amy

I didn't want to feel for anyone else's pain…

$\mathscr{I}$ was not a woman hard up for money because having access to Ricky's accounts was never a problem. For one, my name is and was always on them. However, it was disappointing that the life insurance payouts were being held up. Maybe *frustrating* was a better word. I was the first wife— the rightful wife—the legitimate wife and once everyone recognized that, the kids and I could move on with life.

Going to court to prove who I was didn't seem fair, but I could tell that little Miss Thing with her toddler and newborn was going to present a problem. Instead of handling this with dignity and class—in other words, quietly—she was all over the Internet, responding to questions and allegations much more than what I thought was necessary. And even when she herself wasn't saying anything, it was obvious she had her people and her fans speaking on her behalf.

Iris and her trolls were letting people in on private details. She was the same as every other millennial, living her life out on social media, over-sharing and responding to the most idiotic comments, rumors, and lies. I was mad at myself for even reading the mess that was posted.

Too many days had passed, and I couldn't help but wonder if things were happening that I wasn't privy to. Again, I wasn't desperate for money but if the death certificate and Ricky's body was released to anyone other than me, I was gonna blow a gasket. I took in a few quick breaths, exhaled slowly, and picked up my cell phone.

"Hello, Amy."

"Hey, Rose," I responded, standing in my kitchen. "Is this a good time?"

"Yes, sure. I'm headed to the cafeteria. What can I do for you?"

"I understand the body's been released to you." I opened the refrigerator and removed a jug of orange juice. The kids were still home, and I had prepared breakfast, waiting on them to get out of bed. They would be heading back to school, so it was my last chance to cook for them.

"I don't know where you got that from – it isn't true."

I didn't think it was true, but I wanted to test the waters since I had no idea what was taking so long. I had made many calls to the coroner but not finding out a damn thing. I could hear her breathing heavily.

"Well, the body's been released, right?" I asked her, thinking she definitely knew more than I did.

"Honestly, I have no idea. But, if so, I would imagine he would be coming to you."

"That's what I was thinking but it's taken so long that I thought maybe you, being well-connected and all, maybe intercepted."

"What?"

100

"Yeah…"

"*It doesn't work that way — or, at least not with me. I'm sure you'll hear something soon — I mean, you've already had your memorial service so…*"

"Yes, but I'd still like to bury my husband." I didn't try hard enough not to sound pissed. "Our children need closure."

Rose was silent for a moment.

I had an incoming call and Coach Wagner's name showed on the screen. I ignored the call and continued.

I cleared my throat and adjusted my octave and tone. "Are you there?"

"*Amy, look… I'm sure that like the rest of us, you can't do anything with your insurance policies until there's a death certificate presented — I get that. But, before any of us, you'll be the first to get any informa-tion -- *"

"Sorry I raised my voice. I'm just so stressed — it's been so hard."

"*For all of us…*" her voice remained even keeled.

"And have you seen Iris all over the place, running her mouth?"

"*No, I haven't had time to follow what's going on outside of this hospital.*"

"I have — and that girl is turning this whole thing into a circus. She won't let it die down. She just keeps running her damn mouth. You saw how she was at the hospital that day."

Again, Rose was silent.

I poured OJ in four juice glasses and turned on the coffee maker. I exhaled loudly. "Look, I'm sorry. How are you doing? I mean, I know this is hard for all of us — even her. I mean — I can't believe Ricky screwed us over like this. How did we not see it?"

"*We loved him, that's how.*"

"I didn't know because I refused to see... because believe me, I've known for a long time what he was capable of."

"Actually, I had become suspicious. That's the reason I was initially trying to contact you – to find out if you two were divorced. I had assumed it for years – I mean, I can't actually say I heard him use the word. I think he may have used the term, 'split up' or something like that. I've been thinking back, racking my brain trying to remember and I just can't," her voice cracked a little.

I resisted. I didn't want to feel for anyone else's pain but the kids and mine – no one who came after me, anyway. I was first.

Rose cleared her throat and said, *"At least you and I don't have small children to worry about. You know..."*

"Yeah, I hear you... I still wish she'd exercise some decorum. I mean, come on. This is already feeling like a James Brown situation, taking forever to decide who has the right to bury Ricky."

"Well, if I hear anything on – Rick – the release of the body, I'll let you know," she finally said. *"And I'd appreciate you doing the same – I mean, I'd like to be there when you bury him, if you don't mind."*

"Sure, I'll let you know."

"And it's only fair that Iris be there – the three of us. The whole thing is strange but if you and I are honest, Rick had a life with her just as he had one with both of us. And he started a life with her in recent years so... obviously he wanted to be with her – having babies..." Rose's voice slowed into a whisper. *"She should be there, too."*

We ended our call and I wondered if I would actually let Rose know when I laid Ricky to rest. I damn sure wasn't telling Iris anything.

Sixteen

Rose

None of us deserved it.

$\mathcal{I}$ saw patients, performed surgeries, and handled other hospital business sixteen to eighteen hours per day while I tried sleeping the remainder of those hours. And most of the time that sleep took place at the hospital, which was easier than it would be at home. I missed Rick terribly and enjoying my time at our home just didn't happen anymore. I hoped one day that would change.

In the meantime, I had practically moved into my office and the on-call room, sharing space with other surgeons; sleeping, showering, and dressing there. I knew I wouldn't do that forever, but it was comforting. It was a safe place where I could actually get sleep even if it was only a small amount.

After speaking to Amy, my emotions were all over the place. I wanted to believe that we were all victims of Rick's selfishness and I wanted to disregard any feelings of jealousy I had of Amy and Iris. Knowing that each of them had children to cling to and remember Rick by. They each had pieces of him and I had nothing. I couldn't even call myself a legitimate widow.

I kept pictures of Rick and I on my desk in the office, but I wondered how long I would leave them there. Most of them came from his office once I cleaned it out. There were vacation photos of us on the beach or on a cruise and the two of us at formal events at different times. Not many people came to my office so the shame of me sharing a life with a man that I thought was my husband, for now, was mine alone.

Going through his things was painful but I wanted to do it before Amy or anyone else had. I assumed it wasn't on her radar or she certainly would've done it. All of this was embarrassing but my love for Rick was bigger than the shame he left me with.

I sat at my desk in front of my computer. I hadn't turned it on since the day before Rick died and knew I would be overwhelmed with email messages that I wasn't quite ready to make my way through. I opened my account and responded to or deleted one after another, taking me back to the date of Rick's last day when I came to an email from him. I had completely forgotten about the American Medical Award we were up for when I saw the email he'd forwarded to me.

Rick had responded to the awards committee, answering questions about the patent on our device and phone app for cardiology patients. We were being considered for the Scientific Award focusing on modern technology. He addressed everything, including both of our names and contact information.

I took a moment to download all of the forms just as he'd asked me to in the email. Rick instructed me to keep them all in a safe place. Where I may not have done so right away before, with him gone, I was ever so careful. It was my final piece of him—of us. I knew it was nothing in a practical sense, but it was everything to me. Rick and I didn't just love each other; we loved our work together. So, I clung to the memories of how we would come together, solving problems for our patients.

I printed the papers—there were twelve sheets—placed them in a large envelope, labeled it, and set it next to my purse, ready to go to the bank to be placed in my safety deposit box. The papers weren't really worth all that trouble, but I wanted to treat them as though they were.

I was still so engrossed in clearing away old email messages from my inbox that I didn't hear the knock at the door. But when the door opened, I snapped back to reality.

"Sorry to intrude, Rose. Do you have a moment?" Dr. Patel stood in the doorway.

"Sure, Salem… Please, come in."

I watched him step into the room and close the door.

He stood in front of my desk and made contact with me over the clutter on my desk. "I have a bit of news for you—I figured it couldn't wait."

"Okay, what is it?"

"There's been a decision—I heard. I wanted you to know and not have to wait on them to contact you."

"Rick's body?"

"Yes, he's being released to Amy Hart—I'm assuming his first wife."

I let out a breath and leaned back in my chair. "Yes." I expected it but clearly I was hopeful things had turned out differently.

"She's probably getting a call as we speak. She can have the body moved to her chosen mortuary as soon as today."

"Okay... thanks for letting me know."

"Are you okay?"

I nodded. "I expected it."

"I'm so sorry that Rick left you in this position. You don't deserve it, if you don't mind me saying so."

Tears burned my eyes. I had cried a little but not nearly as much as one would think I had. I sniffed and blinked several times, hoping that would rid me of the inevitable tears.

"*None of us* deserved it."

"Maybe not but you're the only one I know and the only one I know for sure that he loved."

"Yes, well, obviously he loved them, too."

"Well... maybe..." He was stark still. "Please, let me know if I can do anything for you." He ran his hand through his thick dark head of hair, backed up to the door, closing it behind him.

Seventeen

Iris

Goodbye, my love...

$\mathscr{T}$he house was full of people—well, not full but there were plenty of them there offering me support. Everyday there was someone new, but Marigold rarely left my side. Aside from her, there was my publicist and his assistant, a couple of neighbors, and Rasheeda and Garlis from the Mocha Mom's group I belonged to.

I thought after the memorial service the crowds would dissipate, and it did some, but many people lingered. It was nice to have their support even though all I really wanted was time to be alone with my babies.

"Get these people out of here," my mother stood over my shoulder whispering in my ear. "You're gonna be late."

I turned to find her staring me in the eye.

"If you won't do it, I will."

"Iris," Sam called from across the room as he made his way in my direction. "We just got a call from the Wendy Williams Show for an appearance."

"The attorney said we couldn't do anything like that until the estate is settled."

"I know... But how about if Ms. Baldwin prepares the questions? We could at least ask her—this could be the break your career has been waiting for. I'm sorry it's under these circumstances but—"

"No, you're not," my mother spoke up. She turned back to me and said, "God don't like this, Iris."

I understood where she was coming from even though I was getting some satisfaction in the false support their presence seemed to lend.

"It's time for everyone to go. Iris and the kids need rest and they just can't do it with a house full of people." She waved her arms in the air.

The living and dining area grew quiet. I got up on my feet and stood between the two large rooms. "I really do need to rest, you guys." I pulled my hair up and placed it in the ponytail holder I had in the pocket of my jeans.

"So, is that a yes or a no?" Sam asked just as his cell phone buzzed. He took a look at the screen, and then back to me. "We'll get you on a plane to New York day after tomorrow—"

"Marion, I've got this." Marigold winked at my mother and stepped up behind Sam. "I'll let you know Iris's decision by close of business." She took him by the arm, guiding him back to the living area. "Let's give Iris some time to rest, you guys."

I could hear my mother exhale and apparently so could everyone else because all eyes were on her. Soon after, I watched as they all gathered their belongings and moved toward the back door.

Once the house was clear and quiet, Marigold spoke up, "You have two hours to get dressed and get there *and* it's an hour drive."

"Do you want me to go?" my mother asked.

"No, we agreed that it would only be us—no children or anyone. I have to keep my word."

"I'll drive you though," Marigold insisted.

"That's fine but you'll have to wait in the car."

"That's cool—I just don't want you going alone." Marigold added, "You'd better get dressed."

***

Two and a half hours later, Marigold steered my Range Rover onto the grounds of the cemetery. We circled a few minutes before finding the spot where Erick would be laid to rest. Rose had called me the night before and told me the plan. Once Amy had the body released to her, she initially was going to secretly bury Erick but decided to honor Rose's request to be present when it happened. I'm still unclear on how I ended up with an invite. But, in order to come, I had to agree to be alone and to keep my mouth shut so the media wouldn't get wind of it.

I wasn't happy that Erick had been released to Amy. I was told that it was to expedite his burial that the judge ordered him returned to her, but it wouldn't have any bearing on the final court case deciding which of us was the legitimate and rightful wife. I wasn't worried about that.

I left Marigold sitting in the car and made my way across plush green grass, passing headstones and tombstones with every step. I was thirty minutes late and Amy and Rose hadn't waited for me to get started. They were standing in front of the casket when I stumbled close to them. My adrenaline was at an all-time high and it seemed with each step, my heels sunk into the soft ground, causing my ankles to twist and bend.

Both women turned back towards me. Amy held an expression of disgust while Rose gave a slight smile.

"Hey, you made it." Rose stepped over, making room for me.

Amy cleared her throat and dabbed at her eyes with a tissue.

"Sorry, I'm so late," I huffed out.

The casket was a silky black lacquer with gold trimmings and fixtures. White roses sprayed across the top, spilling over the sides. I imagined Erick lying inside and realized the closure I had been eager for had come. I wasn't ready. I thought about my young children never knowing their father and I broke. He was going down in the ground and all would be done. Death was so final. Though I thought I was ready, I wasn't.

The three of us stood in front of the resting place of the man we all thought was our husband. The three of us—each one couldn't be more different from the other: Blond Becky, Mother Earth, and me—Destiny's Child. Clearly, we fulfilled a separate need he had. It was all too much.

My eyes burned with tears when Rose touched my shoulder, pulling me in.

"I'm going to finish." Amy read from a withered piece of paper she held between her pale fingertips. *"Do not remember me as disaster... nor as the keeper of secrets... I am a fellow rider in the cattle cars... watching you move slowly out of my bed... saying we cannot waste time... only ourselves."* She folded her paper, slipped it into her purse's front pocket and blew her nose. "Movement Song by Audre Lorde," she added. "Ricky and I studied her work at Howard." She picked up a single rose from in front of her and turned back to the casket. "Goodbye, best friend... lover... my family..."

Rose and I stood quietly for a moment when Amy sniffed, wiped her nose, turned to us, and spoke up again, "Okay, who's next?"

Rose turned to me and I simply shook my head.

"Okay, well... I don't have anything prepared so I'll just speak from my heart."

A slight breeze brushed my face. It was a gloomy day—not too warm or too cool but definitely gloomy. It was a Wednesday afternoon and it dawned on me I never liked Wednesdays, and this was giving me a new reason to dislike the middle of the week.

I didn't know what the three of us were doing there together. At the time I was being invited, I thought it was a good idea. I needed closure just as they needed it and I knew I wanted to see Erick buried. So, quickly I agreed to come only to find it all awkward. I wanted to hate them—and it was easy to hate Amy but not so easy with Rose. Yes, we were in the same boat—each wondering how this all happened. But, after this, we would all be at odds again.

Rose peered at the closed casket and continued, "Rick, what were you thinking?" She exhaled loudly. "Really, how did this happen—how could you do this? Being angry with you would be so easy right now but what good would it do?" She folded her arms across her upper body. "Instead, I'll simply say that I'm going to miss you and the life we had together... and... I love you. I will always love you."

Rose pulled a single stem from the spray resting on his casket and slowly started to openly cry. She held the rose to her nose, wetting it with her tears.

I felt a knot in my stomach and instantly wished I hadn't come.

"Oh, and congratulations. We won top recognition for the American Medical Award. We did it." Rose spoke to Erick, sniffing and drying her tears. She turned to me again. "Okay, Iris... you have anything you want to say?"

I made eye contact with her and nodded. *Yeah, I have plenty to say.* I searched my mind for a starting point, imagining my format the same way I would if I were writing a blog post. A clear beginning, middle, and end. I would start with our love, fill up the middle with how much Erick loved our children, and end with a sad farewell. I hated that I wasn't prepared.

I opened my mouth and began, "When..." Tears fell. "I..." I shifted my position, inhaled, and wiped my eyes. "The first time I saw you..."

I could hear Amy sound off an irritated moan.

I started again, "The day we married..."

"Look, if you're having a hard time, you don't have to say anything," Amy interrupted.

"Just give her a moment," Rose said to Amy. "Take your time, Iris."

"Take your time? We don't have all day. They gave us an hour and she was thirty minutes late as it is."

"Just give her a minute."

My sorrow turned to anger and I wanted to slap the shit out of Amy. But, instead I blubbered like an idiot. Then, I pulled out a stack of photos and one at a time, I placed them on top of the casket. The first one was of Erick and me on our honeymoon, hugged up on the beach in Cabo. The second picture was of Erick holding Jersey at Sea World with a dolphin soaring in the air behind them. The next one was a

112

professional family picture of the three of us. And finally, I placed a picture of Erick holding Darius in the delivery room next to the others. The only picture they would ever have together.

"Goodbye, my love..." I finally mumbled.

Each photograph haphazardly rested on the bed of flowers, threatening to fly away in the mild wind that was blowing. I would've loved for them to be placed inside with Erick's body, but the casket was closed securely, ready to be lowered into the earth. So, I had to settle with them being loosely placed in the ground. It didn't matter anyway. None of it did, really.

I felt Rose's hand touch my shoulder and some of my tension dissolved. But, before I could settle in —

"Okay, that's the extent of my generosity. I'll see you bitches in court." Amy stepped back, called over the awaiting grounds keepers with the wave of her hand, and headed to her car with her blond hair blowing in the breeze.

Rose nervously turned in my direction. "Are you okay?" she asked me as the men prepared to lower Erick into his final resting place.

"I'll be fine."

We backed away and headed to the road.

"She's hurting just as we are," Rose said as we stepped over headstones pressed into the ground. "Just like you, she's afraid for her children — Rick's children."

My breathing increased as anger took me over. "Don't worry, she's got me fucked up. We'll be ready for her ass in court."

"For the children's sake, I hope it won't come to that — but, that's none of my business."

I stopped in front of the passenger door of my car where Mari sat waiting. "This shit is about to be lit," I said and swung open the door.

Rose gave a simple wave, solemnly shook her head, and kept it moving to her own car parked across the road.

I waved back and got in.

Eighteen

Amy

I needed an escape just for a little while...

$\mathcal{I}$ couldn't believe she tossed all those pictures on Ricky's casket. I should've circled back and had those guys pull them out. But it didn't matter; I had already slipped pictures of Kory, Kylie, and me inside, right under Ricky's folded hands.

Listening to Iris and Rose talk about their lives with my Ricky was too much. How could he do this to me—to us? I kept asking myself if somewhere deep in my consciousness I knew he had been living full lives with other women—or even just with one woman. Did I know and was in denial? Or, was he really that good at juggling separate lives? I felt like a fool and wondered if I'd look less of one if I told people I knew about the other women and we had an open marriage. After all, I'd had lovers of my own. But that just wasn't the way we portrayed ourselves, so it really wouldn't work. And what was the point in trying to save face now? It was all out there for the world to see.

There was no need in harping over the embarrassment; I just needed to get ready for the fight, and I knew Iris and her new babies were going to be the enemy.

Alan greeted me as soon as I came through the back door. The expression on his face told me he had news.

"We have a court date," he announced.

"Good. I'm ready to get this all over with." I placed my purse on the kitchen counter. "It's a shame that I even have to go through this to prove my marital status."

"Well, this is Texas. In another state it would be a bit more cut and dry — not even an issue, really." He marched over to his laptop and turned it towards me. "I know we have an attorney, but I've been doing some of my own research and I've seen some things that concern me."

"Like?"

"If Iris can prove that he publicly acknowledged her as his wife, that could be a problem. Also, if they own anything with both their names on it, that could be a problem."

I exhaled, sat at the kitchen table, and scrolled through Alan's research results. There was a lot there and it was clearly more than my mind had the capacity to grasp at the time. Also, I refused to believe that Iris had any real standing. I wanted to hang on to what I knew in my head and heart. Ricky was my husband only and I was his wife.

"We're meeting with the attorney again tomorrow. We need to prepare."

"I don't know why the facts just don't speak for themselves but that's fine."

"How did it go at the cemetery?" Alan sat across from me.

"Iris tossed pictures of her kids onto the casket, trying to get us to feel sorry for her. Rose fell for it."

"I have to tell you that there is going to be some sympathy for her position. There needs to be a DNA done to make sure the children are Ricky's and if they are, she'll have some rights — or at least the kids will."

"I don't want to think about it right now." I stood and said, "I'm going to lie down."

"We'll talk to the attorney about it tomorrow because I have a lot of questions."

"Okay... whatever... I'm going to bed." I grabbed a bottle from the wine rack and a glass from the cabinet. "Goodnight."

"Sis, you okay?"

"I will be." I held up the bottle and made my way up the stairs.

The journey seemed to take forever. Ricky and I often talked about downsizing our home once the kids were gone, especially since he was rarely there. Yeah, he was rarely home. Now I know why. Well, this big-ass house would be the first thing to go once all of this BS was settled.

Once the double doors were closed, I shed my clothes and ran hot water in the Jacuzzi tub. There was some leftover Ambien in the medicine cabinet, so I disassembled the bathroom in search of it. It wasn't a good idea to wash it down with a Cabernet, but I didn't really care about that. Sleep was all I wanted.

When I found the bottle, I popped two in my mouth — probably should've only had one with the wine — and swallowed them with a palm-full of tap water. I opened the wine and poured a glass full, placing it on the side of the tub just before stepping in.

I sipped and thought—sipped and thought. My mind kept going back to the cemetery and wondered what Ricky would think about the three of us standing over him.

"Do you know the mess you've caused?" I mumbled between sips.

Hearing two women speak about him with such familiarity was difficult, to say the least. He was a husband to each of us, but I would never admit that aloud. I am the one and only wife—the legitimate one—and I kept saying it so there would be no doubt for anyone else. I couldn't help that my husband was unfaithful and any woman with a cheating husband would understand that. I didn't care if Ricky had loved them, he belonged to me.

"Did you see us standing over your casket, Ricky? All of us looking and feeling foolish... I really hate you for this." I poured another glass. "And through all of this, I can't find the love I once had for you—the love I used to feel."

I swallowed that glass in two big gulps and stood up from the water. I poured the last of the wine in my glass, slipped my wet body into Ricky's bathrobe, and made my way to the bed. I had never wanted to get in it as badly as I did at that moment. I needed sleep. I needed an escape just for a little while, and then tomorrow I would be ready to face it all.

Sleep came suddenly but unfortunately I couldn't turn my brain off, still. I couldn't tell if I was saying it aloud, but I kept asking why.

"Why did you do this, Ricky?"

"We weren't supposed to end like this..."

"Why?"

"Baby, I'm sorry," I heard Ricky's voice.

"But, why did you do this to me?"

"None of that matters now. Just know that I love you..."

I know it was a dream, but I felt someone in the room with me, so I opened my eyes. There he was. My Ricky, standing at the foot of the bed.

"You're here..."

"I had to see you – and you needed to see me one last time."

I couldn't find my hate or anger for him. I was well within my right to have my questions answered. I needed to know specifics. I needed to know details: when did he decide to make these other women his family? Was he so unhappy with me that he wanted to start over? Instead, I felt nothing but peacefulness. I couldn't even bring myself to mention the other women.

The intensity of his presence increased as he moved closer to me. I never took my eyes off him even though they were growing heavy. I learned from when my father used to come to me after he died, if I closed my eyes or turned away, he'd disappear. I couldn't let that happen. I wanted Ricky to stay as long as he could.

"I don't want you to worry about what others may say. You come first. Don't worry..."

"We were supposed to grow old together, but you left me."

"I'll never really leave you... I loved you first."

I could barely keep my eyelids up, but I pressed on. "You left a mess."

"Forgive me and try not to blame them. It's not their fault."

"I don't know if I can do that."

"It's all going to be okay."

I felt my eyes closing even though I willed them to stay open. I heard one more 'I love you' from

119

Ricky and it was all over. He was gone. And I was asleep.

I slept hard because it seemed that only moments passed when Alan was knocking on my door to wake me. There was sun beaming through all of the windows, so it was clearly morning. Finally, he came through the door calling my name.

"Are you okay in here?" Alan was fully dressed and placed a cup of coffee on the nightstand next to me.

"Yeah, what time is it?"

"It's nine-thirty and time for you to get up and get it together. Our meeting is at eleven."

I had never felt so down before—even through all of this, this had to be my bottom. I couldn't move. I wanted to go back to what seemed like only moments ago and see Ricky again. I wanted to talk to him and have him tell me again that everything was going to be okay. I knew that once I got out of that bed, the memory of seeing him again would start to fade.

"Come on, get up."

"I'm not going. I'm tired."

"What do you mean you're not going?"

"I can't make it." I pulled the covers up over my head and nestled in.

"You have to be there. Do you want me to reschedule it for later today?"

"No, just go and tell me what's going on when you get back," I announced from under the covers.

"Preliminary court is on Monday. Now is not the time to throw in the towel."

"I'm not—I just can't do it today. Maybe he can ask for a continuance or something."

"A continuance? I thought you wanted this over with quickly."

120

"I haven't even had a chance to grieve the loss of my husband," I yelled, imagining it sounding muffled with the comforter over my head.

"You can't do both. Grieve later and fight now. If you want to make sure those heifas don't get their claws on what's yours, the window of opportunity is now."

"Really..." I poked my head out. "Today is not a good day. Just see if you can relay the information and we'll stay on track with Monday's date."

I heard Alan close the doors behind him once I retreated under the covers again.

Nineteen

Rose

*...I just couldn't look away no matter how
badly I wanted to.*

Opening the mail hadn't been a priority since Rick
died so when I finally spent time at home, and
decided to address household business, I discovered
a letter in a weighted stack of mail, demanding my
appearance in court. My desire to bow out of this
mess gracefully wasn't going to happen. At least not
right away.

I truly wanted to be done with everything and
move on with my life. I could cherish my memories
of Rick without the public humiliation of competing
with women who obviously had the upper hand.
That just wasn't my style.

There wasn't any food in the house, so I managed a cup of tea and some stale graham crackers. I
sat at the breakfast bar holding the letter, reading it
over and over again. I picked up the phone and
scrolled through the contacts, dialing the one
number of whom I knew could help.

"Dr. Rose McDaniel for Stanley Satcher, please."

"Yes, Dr. McDaniel. I'll see if he's available," a voice

on the other end said.

"*Hello, Rose. How are you?*" a new voice said seconds later.

"I'm fine, Stanley. How are you?"

"I'm sorry I couldn't make it to the service. I was out of town. Rick was one of my dearest friends and clients so let me take this moment to extend my sincerest condolences."

"Thank you so much."

"Did you get the flowers Trudy and I sent?"

"Yes, of course. I've been a bit slow about getting out thank you notes."

"No worries. What can I do for you?"

"I have a letter here..." I held it up as if he could see through the phone. "I'm sure you know what's going on... according to this, I'm supposed to appear in court and honestly, I just want to remove myself from the fight. The other two have children — and really, I'm not up to it. I just don't want to put myself through it. Things are ugly enough."

"I doubt if you have a choice but stop by my office and let me see the letter."

"All I need is a death certificate to turn over to the insurance company, you know..."

"I see..."

"Can't you just go in my place and tell the judge I'm bowing out?"

"I can do that for you. But, are you sure that's what you really want?"

"I couldn't be any more sure. Rick and I had a full life together and I don't want to continue to muddy up the memories we shared. There really isn't anything worth fighting for that I don't already have. And as for Amy and Iris, they have good reason."

"What about the house you two lived in?"

"It's my home—I bought it before we moved together. The funny thing is, we had the paper work to add him to the deed, but we never got around to turning them over to the mortgage comp... hey, they can't take my home from me, can they?" Panic arose in my chest. "I mean, he paid the mortgage, but..."

"Well, don't worry about it for now. I'll be there to speak on your behalf. Stop by this afternoon with the letter. It'll be good to see you."

"Thanks, Stanley."

When I disconnected the call, I finished my tea and made my way to the den to lie down for a bit. Sleeping in our bed had proven to be anything but restful. I tossed and turned the night before, dreaming of Rick. The dream was so real I questioned my own sanity once I awakened. It was as if he were in the room with me—speaking to me.

In my dream, Rick looked like himself but more like his *true* self—calm and peaceful. He looked the way I imagine everyone would if they didn't have the weight of the world's trouble resting on them. Not one ounce of stress coming from him. He didn't say much. He mostly smiled; telling me everything would be fine. What I remember most was that he seemed so happy. Not 'laughing' happy but 'satisfied' happy. I was thrilled for him, and everything that I'd been feeling—the anger and disappointment—was nowhere to be found. It only felt good to experience him and his love again.

It was just a dream but in my mind, treated it as if it were real. While tears stung my eyes, I reminded myself of what we were to each other—friends—family. No one could take that from me. But, withdrawal from addiction to Rick was settling in. I didn't recall ever being addicted to anything before, so I was guessing that this is what it must feel like when you can't get the needed fix. My body literally hurt, and my soul was numb. I had no idea how I was going to get through it because working day in and day out would only keep me afloat for so long.

There was enough time for me to rest before preparing to see Stanley, so I turned on the television and wrapped a throw about my shoulders. After clicking through the channels, I settled upon a nationally syndicated talk show. I didn't watch much television, so it was new to me. There were a couple familiar faces of women who sat around a desk—actresses and comediennes. I didn't recognize them all, but I assumed they were all celebrities.

The ladies were discussing what was hot in the media when the subject of the bigamist doctor came up. I could feel a pit forming in my stomach and immediately I wanted to change the station or even turn off the TV. However, I kept listening. It was like a train wreck; I just couldn't look away no matter how badly I wanted to.

Amy, Iris, and I were called every ugly name imaginable—as well as stupid. "How dumb were these women?" one woman asked. She went on to say that she knew her husband's every move so that situation could never happen to her. Another woman berated her co-hosts of bashing women and letting the man off the hook. "Why is no one going ham on him?" she asked. 'Ham' was a new term for me.

I found it interesting that people were arguing over the mess we were in. Some called all three of us stupid, some called Rick a womanizer, and most everyone sympathized with Amy—everyone except most black women. And then, when it came out that she too was a black woman, there was a debate over whether or not it was true, and why it mattered if she was or wasn't.

There was also plenty of discussion on Iris because she was already a bit of a celebrity in her own right and there were plenty of photos and video footage of her and her work. Then, there was talk of her losing endorsements because of the scandal. My heart broke for her. She had children to raise so I didn't know how she was dealing with all of her attention being pulled in different directions. She got most of the heat because she was the last woman to come aboard and most thought she was a mistress ignoring that the 'good doctor' was married.

The insults hurled in my direction, I felt, were thrown in for good measure. I was, apparently, some skank doctor likened to the fictional ones on "Greys Anatomy" and other such television shows. Clearly, I needed to watch more TV because I had no idea to what they were referring. And just viewing the bit that I had, it was easy to see how people with nothing to do could get caught up, tuning in day after day. Maybe it was because my real life was being discussed but those few minutes left me exhausted with the yelling, screaming, and snappy comebacks being hurled across the studio.

With tears still burning my eyes, I hit the off button and headed to the shower.

Twenty

Iris

... three trusting and stupid bitches.

So much had happened leading up to the trial that I had lost track of where we were. There had been preliminary court dates and lots of preparation with Greta outlining our strategy. On one hand I was exhausted and on the other, I couldn't rest or walk away.

Since Rose had made it clear that she wanted no parts of the fight, she had never shown up to any of the court dates. However, her attorney was in attendance every time, taking notes while saying very little. Judge Long wouldn't let her completely remove herself from the proceedings but he couldn't do anything about her refusing to fight or defend herself. For me, it was one less person for me to go against, so I didn't care. I imagine neither did Amy.

I met Greta in the hall outside of the courtroom. I towered over her small, rotund frame as she did her best to calm me while keeping me ready for a fight. Amy would be presenting her position today, so we would mostly be listening to her attorneys. Marigold and my mother were already seated inside.

Greta said she felt good about the case we would be presenting, and I trusted her. All sides agreed to forgo a trial by jury, so the judge alone would be making the decision. I took a deep breath, said a quick prayer, and followed her inside. I waved in the direction of my mother and Marigold and took my seat.

Amy was at the table to the left of us. Her team of "Johnnie Cochran" attorneys surrounded her with one of them clearly being the lead. There was another man with her, too, who I was told was her brother. There was no mistaking him for being Caucasian the way most people mistook her. He was tall, handsome, and like the men on that side of the room, dressed as if he was going to be on the cover of the next *GQ* Magazine.

I tried my best not to feel intimidated, nor regret my choice in attorney, but in a room full of men, Greta, the only woman, was unattractive and small in stature. She certainly did not command attention the way I would have liked.

Once the bailiff brought order to the courtroom, Judge Long entered and took her place and asked everyone to be seated. The room was full, and I was certain that some of them were the media, taking notes, ready to rush out and report the happenings.

"Thank you all for being here," Judge Long said, pushing her glasses up on her face. She appeared to be in her late 50s and I silently hope that she and Greta had a good track record. The last thing I needed was to have two women with bad blood working against me, and my interests. "We're here to determine the legitimate wife of Dr. Erick Eugene Hart. The litigants, Amy Hart, Iris Hart, and Dr. Rose McDaniel—Mr. Satcher, will Dr. McDaniel be in attendance today?"

"No, Your Honor. As previously discussed, she is not staking any claim. I'm here to speak on her behalf since you won't let her completely recuse herself." Rose's attorney sat alone with a note pad at the table to the right of me.

"That's fine but keep in mind that she will need to be present for the verdict."

"Not a problem."

The judge turned her attention to the other end of the courtroom. "Mr. Blankenship, are you ready to give your opening statement?"

"Yes, Your Honor." Amy's attorney stood to his feet.

Greta opened several folders in front of her and clutched a pen, ready to take notes. I mimicked her actions pulling out a notepad from my designer bag next to me.

"Your Honor, Amy Hart—*Mrs.* Amy Hart met Dr. Erick Hart before he was Dr. Hart—in fact, while the two of them were young students at Howard University in nineteen-eighty..." Mr. Blankenship paced in front of the judge, making off and on eye contact with her. "...they met, fell in love, and married five years later. Not only did Amy help support him and their growing family while he finished medical school, but she has never left his side since the day they married. They have two beautiful children—a son and daughter, twenty-year-old Kory and eighteen-year-old Kylie and like any other married couple, have had their fair share of ups and downs—but mostly up."

Mr. Blankenship made a dramatic pause in front of Amy, stared at her for a moment before continuing, "Amy remained to be a dedicated wife to Dr. Hart until the day he died. They shared a home in Sherman, Texas and even though he was a man devoted to his profession as a doctor, remained happily married with a full life as a couple." He stood in front of the judge. "We will show in these proceedings today that Ricky, as Amy affectionately calls him, and Amy Hart were a loving couple committed to one another, living as a family and that she alone is the first... the original... and the *only* legitimate Mrs. Hart."

Judge Long waited for him to return to his seat. She was clearly writing on something in front of her, and then turned to Greta. "Ms. Baldwin, you have the floor."

I paid close attention to the chemistry between the two women and all seemed normal.

Greta quickly jotted a few last notes and then stood to her feet. "Thank you, Your Honor." With her orthopedic shoes squeaking on the hardwood floors, she marched in front of the awaiting spectators.

"Iris Hart met a man in an airport," Greta started. "Not just any man but a doctor who she witnessed save a fellow passenger's life. From the moment she met him, treating her to lunch and cocktails while they waited on their connecting but separate flights, he consistently presented himself as a man free to pursue her, telling her he had been estranged from his wife for ten years. The year was two thousand and twelve. He courted her, they fell in love, and after he proposed, they had a beachside wedding with their friends and loved ones. It isn't relevant that Iris is a young wife and mother—Jersey four years old, a sweet and prissy little girl—and Darius a newborn baby boy who will never know the father that was excited about his arrival and was there when he was born and the first to hold him when he took his first breath. That's not what we'll focus on in this case."

Greta stopped pacing long enough to take in a slow breath, and then faced only Judge Long. " What is relevant is that, in these proceedings, I will show that not only was Dr. Erick Hart legally married, dedicated, and devoted to his family with Iris, I will show that he was not acting as husband in any way shape or form with either of the litigants — Amy Hart or Dr. McDaniel. There is only one wife here and that is the last woman doctor Hart said 'I do' to. Thank you."

I felt myself exhaling when Greta came my direction. My confidence was returning with every squeaky step should took.

Amy's team seemed to scoff during Greta's opening but she, in turn, seemed to pay it no mind. When she plopped down next to me, she opened a large folder and organized her papers.

"Mr. Blankenship," Judge Long said.

Amy's attorney stood to his feet and replied, "My first witness is Kory Hart."

One of the members of their team escorted Amy's son through the doors. Wearing khaki pants and a white button-down Polo shirt, he looked so much like Erick, aside from having Amy's blue eyes. It was startling. I held my composure, but tears burned my eyes.

Kory stepped into the witness stand, was sworn in, and took a seat. He was visibly nervous, which afforded him sympathy right away. Amy dabbed at a tear, real or fake I didn't know, and then blew her nose.

"Hello, Kory," Mr. Blankenship started. "First, let me offer condolences on the loss of your father."

"Thank you," Kory politely responded. I was happy to see that he seemed to be such a mannerable young man—reminding me more and more of Erick with every word he spoke.

"I'm sorry that you have to do this but answer honestly and to the best of your recollection."

Kory nodded.

"Kory, you will need to speak all of your answers, okay?" Judge Long interjected.

"Yes, Your Honor."

"Kory, when was the last time you spoke to your father?"

"The week before he died. But, he called me two days before he died and I hadn't gotten a chance to call him back," Kory's voice cracked.

"When you did speak to him, what did you two talk about?" Mr. Blankenship leaned against the witness booth.

"Well, he just asked me how school was going—he always gave me advice on classes and how to handle professors—and he wanted to know if I was planning on working through the summer because he wanted all of us to take a family vacation. Last summer was the first summer in many years that we didn't all take one and he wanted to make up for it."

"That's nice. Where did he mention you all might spend that vacation?"

Kory breathed in, obviously trying to maintain his composure and finally answered, "One year, I think I was about sixteen and Kylie, my sister, was fourteen." He paused and began again, "Mom and Dad took us to Disney World. We didn't want to go—I mean my sister and me—thinking Disney was for little kids. So, we had really bad attitudes about it. But, it turned out to be the best family trip we'd ever taken. So, my dad mentioned maybe we would make that trip again — to Disney World."

"I'm sorry that wasn't able to happen for you all."

Kory simply nodded his head, and then glanced over at the judge and added, "Yes, sir."

"So, when was the last time you actually saw your father?" Blankenship asked.

"At Christmas when I was home from school."

"Did you, your mother, and sister spend Christmas day with your father?"

"Of course. It was a great day — a good Christmas."

"Do you remember what gifts you received?"

"No — I think money and clothes — I'm not sure. My mother usually did all of the shopping and the cash would come from Dad."

"Okay. Thank you for your testimony, Kory." Blankenship headed back to his team.

"You're welcome."

"Ms. Baldwin, any cross examining for this young man?"

Greta surprised me by standing and saying, "Yes." She had initially told me she wouldn't question the children because she thought it could backfire.

"Kory, let me also extend my condolences on the loss of your father," Greta started.

Kory didn't respond, and I was nervous about her continuing.

"On this past Christmas when you and your sister were home from school, did your father wake up with the family on Christmas morning?"

"I don't remember."

"Well, was he there the night before, on Christmas Eve?"

"I was out with friends so I'm not sure — actually, I don't think so. I guess he was at the hospital."

"So, is it possible that he hadn't been home all night but came to the house Christmas morning to open gifts?"

"It's possible — like I said he may have been at the hospital. He spent a lot of time there seeing after his patients."

"I'm sure he did, son." Greta took a few steps. "So, how long was your Christmas break — how long were you home?"

"About a month or so — maybe six weeks."

"Out of all those days you were home, how many days would you say your father spent nights at home with you, your sister, and mother?"

"I'm not sure. My dad slept at the hospital a lot."

"Is it possible that he didn't sleep at home even one time during that period?"

"No, there were times we all woke up in the house and had breakfast together — but my dad has always had odd hours and long hours of being at the hospital," he said with frustration etched in his tone.

"Yes, I'm sure that's true, Kory."

"My dad lived there. All of his clothes and things was at our house."

"Do you ever remember a time when your parents talked about or considered getting a divorce?"

"No, never," there was a clear exclamation in Kory's voice. But, it wasn't clear if he was telling the truth.

"Thank you for your testimony, son," Greta said as sweetly as she could.

I was nervous about the approach she was taking. I didn't like seeing Kory upset. But, I decided to trust that Greta knew what she was doing.

"Mr. Blankenship?" Judge Long said.

"No re-cross examine at this time, Your Honor."

Kory glanced over at the judge and stood only after getting her approval.

"You're excused for now," Judge Long responded.

Once Kory was escorted out of the courtroom, the proceedings resumed.

I was glad that Kory didn't lie about Christmas morning because Erick was home with Jersey and me, rubbing my swollen belly all night. It's obvious now that he lied when he told me he had to go check on a patient and made a beeline to Amy's house.

Yeah, we were three trusting and stupid bitches.

Twenty-One

Amy

...the reason we're all here now.

$\mathcal{I}$ first told Alan that I wouldn't testify, answering questions about the intimacies of my marriage. But, the morning of the trial, I changed my mind and in their frustration, the attorneys did their best to prepare me for questioning. They wanted to get a continuance, but I assured them I was ready. None of it would be a problem — all I had to do was tell the truth. Easy.

When the young attorney, one of the men on the team of attorneys Alan hired, called me to the stand, I spoke in the most colorful language I could muster up. I explained how Ricky and I met, fell in love, and rushed to be married. I even detailed our June wedding day and how on every five years on our anniversary, Ricky updated my wedding ring with a new ring or an additional diamond. This year would mark another five years and I presented proof my husband had been researching rings.

Using some modesty, I even described our sex life and the last time we made love, detailing the day we spent together, celebrating my latest cosmetic surgery. Even when I was asked about any infidelity in the marriage my simple response was that I was married to a handsome doctor so there had been times over the years when he gave into the temptation of the many women throwing themselves at him. He was a red-blooded man but always made it clear he wasn't going anywhere. We always worked through our problems. There was no doubt we were still together and that *was* the truth.

Iris's attorney declined cross-examining me but asked the judge for permission to recall me later if it proved to be necessary. She was crazy if she thought she was going to trick me into helping prove her case, so I wasn't intimidated at all. I looked forward to it.

The attorneys also called our housekeeper. Her testimony didn't go as well since she mostly corroborated that Ricky was rarely home. I wasn't worried because it was made clear that she was only at the house twice a month since the kids left home. There were also neighbors and some of Ricky's long-time patients, turned family friends, who were there to support us.

When we were done calling witnesses, Iris's lopsided attorney stood and requested that we break for lunch because she was waiting on a witness to arrive. She said the witness was leaving work and would be ready to testify in an hour.

I think we all were relieved and needed a break and something to eat so Judge Long gave us an hour and a half.

Alan, Kory, and me made our way to Perry's Steak House, relaxed, and enjoyed a five-star meal. It was what we needed — an escape and good food. It seemed no sooner than we settled in, it was time to get back to the courthouse, so we did just that.

Blankenship told Kory that he would no longer be needed to testify and sent him home.

I hugged him in the hallway. "Thank you for your honesty, sweetie. I know it wasn't easy sitting up there."

"I see why you refused to let Kylie testify. I don't think she could've handled it." Kory tightly embraced me and simply replied, "I love you, Mom."

"I'll see you home later."

He then turned and left the courthouse.

I headed to the ladies' room, passing Iris as she was coming through the doors. We exchanged hateful glances. She swung her unbeweaveable hair over her shoulder and her towering statuesque body breezed by me.

When court resumed, it was just as we had left off. Rose's attorney sat alone, Iris and her low-budget lawyer were at the other table and my dream team was with me. There was some slight bustling in the room until the bailiff, once again, called it to order.

Everyone stood and waited for Judge Long to take her seat. I was so ready to get it all over with I really didn't plan to pay much attention to Iris's side present their case. What could she possibly say? Aside from being Ricky's mistress who had his children out of wedlock, she meant nothing.

"Ms. Baldwin, I assume your witness has arrived."

I heard the squeaking from Ms. Baldwin's shoes, indicating she was ready to begin presenting her case.

"Yes, Your Honor but I would first like to call Iris Hart to the stand."

The raving beauty, looking too young for a man Ricky's age, floated to the witness stand wearing a houndstooth suit and red patent leather stiletto pumps. Her short skirt made her appear as Ricky's seductress. I was glad she was helping to prove my point.

Ms. Baldwin asked leading questions that allowed Iris the opportunity to go on and on about her so-called magical romance with *my* husband. Most of the time I zoned out but the parts I did hear pierced my heart and soul.

My confidence had faded and only continued when her attorney showed a video of their beachside destination wedding with the two of them barefoot in the sand with their white linen blowing in the wind. Ricky looked so happy that I had to turn away.

There were more videos. Vacation videos. Videos of their daughter being born. Videos of their son being born — Ricky was there cheesing from ear to ear each time. There were Christmases, Easter Sundays, and other holiday videos added to the home movie marathon. And unlike any evidence we had, there was even a video of Ricky waking up in their bed on Christmas morning and the two of them waking up their daughter to open gifts. It wasn't just that last video, but I had no idea that anyone kept such tangible records of their daily lives and I couldn't imagine Ricky being comfortable with any of it.

Mr. Blankenship only cross-examined Iris after I insisted he asked her something.

"Miss Hart—"

"That's Mrs.," Iris responded and sat up straight in her seat, tossing that damn hair again.

"Okay, Mrs. Hart, when you first met Dr. Hart in the airport as you described, you didn't suspect that he might be a married man?"

"Actually, I did."

"And so how did you conclude that he wasn't married, or was it that it didn't matter to you if he were?"

"Of course it mattered. But, he wasn't wearing a wedding band so..."

"So... because he wasn't wearing a wedding band, you thought he wasn't married?"

"One, he wasn't wearing a wedding band and two, he asked that we keep in touch. Why would I think he was married?"

"Do you think that was naive of you? I mean, now that you know he was married."

"I still don't believe he was married and everything he ever said to me led me to believe he was divorced—or he thought he was anyway." Iris looked in my direction.

"Tell me, did you ever, in the time that you knew Dr. Hart, ask him straight out if he were, in fact, divorced?"

"Of course—well, I don't know if I asked but the word was certainly spoken—and spoken in that context."

"By you or by him?"

There was a pause, and then finally Iris answered, "I honestly don't remember."

"Thank you."

That was it. I was disappointed that she wasn't shaken up at all. It wasn't what I expected at all. I wanted her to be a flustered, frustrated blubbering idiot. But, she was cool and direct. There was no way she looked like the desperate side piece in denial about her man being married to another

143

woman while she crept around with him—waiting for him to show up once he could sneak away from his family. No, she wasn't that chick.

Iris's attorney called her personal assistant to the witness stand next. Her name was Marigold Jones and for whatever reason, her name seemed to fit her. She wore braids and wire-framed glasses and yoga pants with a turtleneck.

"Miss Jones," Ms. Baldwin started. "How long have you worked for celebrity blogger, Iris Hart?"

"Three years, maybe three and a half."

"Did you have a chance to meet Dr. Hart, her husband?"

"Yes, on many occasions."

"Oh, so you knew him?"

"Yes, of course."

"Where would you see him mostly?"

"At their home—that's where we worked mostly. So, that's where I would see him."

"How often would you see him there?"

"I don't know—if I had to give a percentage, it would be about fifty percent of the time that I was there."

"That much?"

"Maybe a little less. He was mostly at the hospital, I presume."

"Sure—sure." Ms. Baldwin paced with that annoying squeaking coming from her shoes. "So, when was the last time you saw Dr. Hart, Miss Jones?"

"I think it was the day Iris went into labor. He was about to take her to the hospital when I showed up at their home."

Ms. Baldwin turned to the judge, "I'd like to play exhibit twelve."

Judge Long nodded her approval just before the next video came on to the screen.

"Is this the day you're talking about, Miss Jones?"

The footage appeared to be a cellphone video and it became apparent that Iris was the one filming. It was her face on the screen and there was a lot of moving about. I could hear Ricky's voice in the background, asking her to turn off the video when suddenly, the view switches and Marigold comes through the door. She clearly asks Ricky, 'where's your wife' and he answers her by pointing to Iris.

It was the final knife in my chest. That final bit of hope that I didn't even know I was holding on to, was dashed. I could feel my pale skin grow warm and I knew it was ruby red. I completely checked out while Ms. Baldwin continued to question Iris's assistant. I didn't want to hear anymore.

There were several other people parading the witness stand: their neighbors, babysitters, and the like. I had no idea what any of them said.

And then...

I heard Ms. Baldwin call one more name, but I thought I was surely mistaken. I waited to see if she would repeat herself, but she didn't. I turned with everyone else to see who was going to come through the doors and my heart dropped when he did. It was Coach Wagner.

I imagine my eyes were wide as saucers. I kept trying to blink but couldn't.

Coach was dressed as if he had just come from the school—sweat pants, knit shirt complete with a whistle hanging around his neck. He stepped into the witness stand and waited for the bailiff to approach.

"Please, state your name."

"David Wagner," he answered.

"Do you swear to tell the truth, the whole truth, and nothing but the truth, so help you, God?"

"I do."

I still hadn't blinked.

Ms. Baldwin started her squeaky saunter across the floor and got right to it. "Thank you for being here, Coach Wagner," she said.

"Are you okay?" One of the attorneys on my team asked me. I hadn't taken the time to learn their names and I then regretted not being more involved. They had presented me with a list of witnesses and I never read it.

I didn't answer. I simply removed a fan from my purse, opened it, and cooled myself off.

"You're welcome," David answered Ms. Baldwin.

I hadn't answered the many calls or texts he'd made trying to reach me. I had fully decided to wait to return them when all the drama had subsided and was planning to pick up where we'd left off.

Why was he here? Who brought him here? Or, did he contact them telling them he had juice to help their case? His testimony could totally make me look like a woman who had moved on from her marriage, so I just held my breath and tried to pay attention.

"Coach Wagner, can you tell the court how you know Mrs. Amy Hart?" she asked him.

David cleared his throat, still not looking my direction, and said, "Yes, Amy and I have been in a relationship for the past five years."

There was some mumbling in the courtroom and Blankenship turned to look at me.

I finally blinked.

Five years? I couldn't believe he lied like that.

"When you say relationship, what do you mean by that?"

"I mean a romantic relationship—we were dating, you know, seeing each other."

"Was this romantic relationship sexual? Were you two intimate?"

That's when David's eyes met mine but only for a brief moment.

"Yes, we were—*are* intimate." He shifted a bit in his seat.

"You say *are*, so does that mean you are currently in a relationship with Mrs. Hart?"

"With everything that's going on we haven't seen each other but yes."

"What about Dr. Hart? What was your impression of the relationship between them?"

"Objection," Blankenship finally spoke up. "The witness's impression about the relationship of a married couple is irrelevant. We don't even know who this man is, Your Honor."

"I'll allow it," Judge Long responded.

"Go ahead, Coach Wagner," Ms. Baldwin said.

"I was under the impression that they were divorced but still friends."

I couldn't believe it. As David's testimony continued, he told lie after lie, making it seem as if he and I had much more than what we really did. Was he so angry with me for not calling him back that he would lie in such a way? He lied about everything. Yes, he knew my kids but that was from school when they were students, but he made it seem like my children knew about he and I being together. I was totally humiliated.

It had only been a few moments, but it seemed as though it went on forever. I was so caught up in the things he said that I didn't even see him leave the courtroom nor did I hear Ms. Baldwin recall me as a witness. I almost fainted. And then, I could see the satisfied expression on Iris's face, so I regained my composure and took my place.

"Please be reminded that you are still under oath, Mrs. Hart," Judge Long stated.

"Yes, ma'am." I straightened out my clothes and smoothed my hair.

"Mrs. Hart, knowing that you are under oath—"

"I know I'm under oath," I spat out.

"Good. How long have you been sleeping with your son's former coach?"

I choked but got it together quickly. "David and I flirted with one another for years, but I will admit that I had stepped out on my marriage for the first time ever, earlier this year. It was one time and one time only. I swear." I didn't know if that admission helped or hurt the case, but I just didn't have time to think.

"So, you had this devoted husband in Dr. Hart and you flirted with another man for years and then finally gave in to that flirting and slept with a man that wasn't your husband?"

I said nothing.

"Did Dr. Hart know you cheated on him?"

"Ricky cheated on me for years and I had just this one slip up," I defended myself.

"Dr. Hart cheated on you for years?"

"Yes, he did."

"With how many other men did you cheat on your husband?"

"None."

"So, is the court supposed to believe you now—you and Dr. Hart were happily married but cheated on each other—or earlier that you were both devoted to each other and only each other? Which one is it?"

"Look, it isn't the way David said at all. He knew I was a married woman and that was a one-time thing. I loved my husband and he loved me even though over the years I caught him seeing other women to the point where I just decided to stop looking for evidence of him cheating. That's probably the reason we're all here now."

"Did Dr. Hart know you were in a relationship with another man?"

I felt tears burning my eyes when I answered, "He suspected but he never knew who... or any details."

"Is that because in reality, you and he had been estranged for a long time — possibly years?"

"No. It was because I hadn't told him, and I imagine at some point I would have."

"I have nothing else, Your Honor." Ms. Baldwin squeaked her way back to her seat.

My attorneys redirected, asking me to clarify my relationship with David but none of it helped. The damage had been done.

Closing remarks only proved to prolong the inevitable. I felt that I had lost the case and I was frustrated because I realized my own negligence in fighting. And there were no do-overs. And the closing remarks were a reminder of that very fact.

The only things my attorneys could focus on in closing were that I was the first Mrs. Hart and there was no divorce or evidence of a divorce. Iris's attorney not only made it clear that Iris was the last woman Ricky had said 'I do' to and his apparent excitement and involvement in his children's births showed that he claimed Iris as his current wife.

BIGAMIST

To add insult to injury, Ms. Baldwin reminded the judge that Ricky and I had no marriage to speak of in recent years and the fact that I had moved on with my life with another man proved I knew there was no marriage.

A smug Iris and I made eye contact for a moment just as the judge laid down the gavel, closing the proceedings. She and I both knew how this thing was going. I lowered my head, joined my brother, and exited the courtroom.

Twenty-Two

Rose

> *I wanted to say something to*
> *Amy and Iris but...*

$\mathcal{E}$very day I worked hard at avoiding the news. I didn't want to know what was going on with the trial and there seemed to be nothing but updates and breaking commentary. Those closest to me knew to avoid the subject.

The hospital was where I felt closest to Rick, so I spent all of my time there. Not even our home made me feel his presence the way the Presby corridors did. But the day had come when I had to rid myself of my daily uniform of scrubs and lab coat, to put on a skirt and blouse to appear in court.

I didn't really understand why it was necessary for me to be present for the verdict but the last thing I wanted to be was in contempt of court. I told myself it would be the last hurtful thing I would have to face where Rick was concerned and then I could move on with my life. I just needed to get this over with.

Anxious to do just that, I marched into the courthouse forty-five minutes early. I was clearly the first one there because there was no media to be found. So, I quietly waited on a bench out front, doing my best to blend in. Stanley showed up not too much later to escort me in. He found a room we could hide out in until we could enter the courtroom.

"There's no need to be nervous, Rose. This should all go smoothly and quickly."

"Which way do you think it's going to go?" I asked. I couldn't help but be curious.

"I have to tell you, the young woman with the newborn has a pretty good case and that attorney of hers, Greta Baldwin, is a known beast in the courtroom. It's hard to say. Judge Long is fair but Texas has some quirky marital laws — this will be interesting for sure."

"I don't envy either of them — they both must be concerned for their children. I guess that's one blessing in all of this for me. I don't have to bear that burden."

The sound of traffic in the hallways grew louder. I peaked at my watch and time was drawing near. We slipped out of the room and headed in the direction of the courtroom.

We could see the media frenzy over the banister on the first floor at the front doors before entering the courtroom.

"I guess the other defendants are arriving," he said.

"Is this how it's been?"

"Pretty much — but today, the verdict coming in even has national attention."

I didn't want to even think about it. I wondered just how bad the punishment would be if I ducked out of there. Instead, I sat quietly and waited.

Suddenly we hear screaming and cursing and what sounded like tussling coming from the other side of the doors. Stanley, and a few others who were on the other side of the room, trickled out to the hallway to find out what was happening. The doors finally opened, and people quickly filled the room.

I did my best to keep my attention to the front of the room; not looking around, knowing that the people were there only to get a glimpse of the third foolish woman who had no idea her husband was married to other women. Like one of the talk show hosts said in reference to us not knowing about each other, 'Texas ain't that damn big!'

Amy was the first of the other two to make her entrance. She was dressed in a powder blue pantsuit that matched her eyes beautifully. It was obvious that she wasn't in the mood to exchange pleasantries, so I didn't even try to be cordial. I could see her straightening out her clothes and smoothing down her hair. She was breathing hard and was clearly and understandably unhappy about being in court. Several men, I assumed her attorneys, surrounded her, asking if she was okay.

Moments later, security escorted Iris and her attorney through the doors. She was dressed to kill in all white, which looked great on her chocolate skin. Her presence demanded attention and I was certain that her whole ensemble and look was all planned. Iris expected to be victorious, and according to my attorney, it was looking good for her. However, she, too, stormed in as if the Dallas County Courthouse was the last place she'd rather be. Again, understandable.

All three of us looked as if we wished this nightmare would just end.

Stanley rejoined me at the table. "Iris and Amy had an altercation out in the hallway," he told me.

"Physical?"

Stanley simply nodded, and I then shook my head and held it down.

Once the bailiff called the room to order, we were instructed to stand until Judge Long entered and took her seat. She did so with a poker face in place.

I had every intention to observe the happenings and that was it, so I adopted her same poker face, barely breathing and moving. I didn't want to bring any attention to myself.

Judge Long looked around the room and slowly opened her mouth. "First let me say that I am deeply disappointed. The two of the three defendants here—the two that happen to be mothers, reduced themselves to a brawl out in the hallway as if they were in an alley." She peered at Amy and Iris. "What example are you setting for your children? And let us not forget that a man is at the bottom of all this. He's the reason you all are even here—he deceived each of you. Yet, instead of having some dignity and seeing this for what it really is, you turn on each other instead of directing your anger to the right person."

The whole courtroom was quiet when Amy scoffed.

"And Amy Hart, you should be setting the example." Judge Long settled back in her seat. "I would only hope that when all of the emotions die down, you two will make an effort for these children, who are siblings, to get to know one another."

I simply held my head down.

"Let's move on... deciding who is the legitimate wife of Dr. Erick Hart comes down to which of you he claimed as his wife last, just prior to his death.

There is no question whom he married first, nor is there any question he was with all three of you, acting as a husband. So, I'm going to do something that I just decided this morning and ask Dr. Rose McDaniel to take the witness stand."

There was some rustling in the room and I turned my attention to Stanley. He simply hunched his shoulders.

"I realize that you wanted to recuse yourself from these proceedings and forgo any claims that may involve you, but it just isn't as simple as that. Please, come forward and be sworn in."

So much for wanting to blend into the crowd; I slowly stood to my feet and took my place in the witness stand. Once I was sworn in, I took a seat and turned to the judge.

"Dr. McDaniel, is it true that you and Dr. Hart were never married in front of a judge or minister?"

"Yes, that's true."

"Why is that?"

"Well..." I blinked a few times. "He wanted to get married, in fact, he asked me many times. But, I have never fully embraced the whole thing of having a contract on another person. I believe that if you love each other, you take care of each other. No court system should have to be involved in that, making a person do the right thing."

"How long did the two of you live together under one roof?"

"We lived together seven years."

"Did you know he was married to either of these ladies during the time you were together?"

"I didn't know about Iris at all until after he died. But, just before he died, I suspected that he had not had a legal divorce from Amy and I asked him about it."

"How did he respond?"

"We were supposed to talk about it the day he died. In fact, I was on my way to see him to discuss it but when I arrived..." my voice trailed off. "I found him unconscious."

The bailiff placed a box of tissues next to me.

"I'm sorry," Judge Long said.

"But, to answer your question, he never admitted to still being married but I had also tried contacting Amy, but we played phone tag and didn't get a chance to talk until after he — was gone."

"When was the last time you spoke to Dr. Hart?"

"Earlier that morning, April tenth. We were home — I made breakfast and we ate."

"What was the last public correspondence the two of you had?"

"I'm not sure I know what you mean, Your Honor."

"Your Honor, if I may," Stanley spoke up. "There was an email he copied her on, mere moments before he collapsed." He shuffled through a folder in front of him, finally holding it up in the air.

"Let's enter this in as evidence," Judge Long said to a clerk before turning to the bailiff. "Hand the witness the letter, please."

Once I had the paper in my hand, I began to shake.

"Read the letter aloud, please."

With my hands shaking, I held the letter up. "Dear Committee Members of the American Medical Society, thank you for your consideration of the scientific award you have extended to my wife, Dr. Rose McDaniel and myself for our patent-pending medical device. We are humbled, as well as excited, to accept the nomination for this prestigious award. We have, in fact, completed the additional documentation required by your organization and will be in attendance at the ceremony in the fall. Please, find the signed documents attached to this email and let us know if there is anything further you need from us. Sincerely, Doctor Erick Hart, MD Cardiologist Specialist." I peered over the paper to catch a glimpse of Judge Long, hoping to understand what relevance this all had on these proceedings.

"What date was this email sent?" Judge Long asked me.

"April tenth, mere moments before he died. In fact, I didn't see that he'd copied me on the email until days—or even a week after it was sent."

"Thank you. You can take your seat."

I did as she instructed all the while, and with every step, wondering what had just happened.

"None of this is easy. For all of you involved, I'm sorry that you're here, having to go through this because I don't think any of you were negligent. You were just trusting women in love with a man. There is no dispute that Dr. Hart married Amy Hart first, in the interim, he takes up a home with Rose McDaniel. He then, marries and starts a family with Iris Hart. Dr. Hart was fortunate enough to find three women who didn't ask enough questions until it was too late. With that said, the laws in Texas are peculiar and allow for conditions not found in other states. Common law marriage has mostly the same legal strengths as a union performed in a courthouse or a wedding chapel with a marriage license. Iris is the last woman he made his wife; however, I have to consider which of you was the last woman he claimed as his wife. And based on the evidence presented here today, I am awarding Doctor Rose McDaniel as the legitimate wife of Doctor Erick Hart and all that the title entails with the full extent of the law. If there is nothing else, this case is closed, and the proceedings adjourned."

I couldn't believe it. I never saw this coming and it was clear that neither did Amy or Iris. I reluctantly glanced over at the two of them and they were both stone-faced and in a state of shock.

The media went crazy, rushing outside of the courtroom to hopefully be the first to break the news.

I turned to Stanley and he simply smiled, stood to his feet, and helped me to mine. We were all caught off guard. He took me by the elbow and escorted me through the double doors.

I wanted to say something to Amy and Iris but decided Stanley may know best and continued to follow him. I wanted them to know that I, in no way, was expecting what happened and that I would do everything to make sure they had death certificates to claim their own insurance policies.

"What are your plans now, Doctor McDaniel?"

"Are you going to help out the other two defendants and their children?"

"What do you have to say to the mothers of your dead husband's children?"

Stanley stood in front of the gang of reporters, with me next to him, and spoke, "Obviously, we were not expecting this verdict but we're very pleased at the outcome. Doctor McDaniel will need time to digest the judge's decision so there is no comment at this time. Thank you."

Stanley stuffed me into the passenger side of his SUV. "We'll have your car picked up later. Let's get out of here."

***

One week later.

I was the last to arrive at Stanley's office, but I was glad to see that Amy and Iris were there calmly waiting.

"Please forgive me for being late." I took the only empty seat at the conference table."

Stanley spoke up, "We realize we could've simply mailed copies of the death certificate to you both, but Rose wanted to clear the air and answer any questions you may have—against my advice, I might add."

Amy folded her arms across her chest and Iris's expression was deadpan.

I spoke up, "I know that the three of us will never be friends, but it would be nice if we could just be friendly, especially the two of you for the sake of the children. But I wanted to say once more that I was as surprised as anyone with the judge's verdict. I also want to make it clear that I will not come after anything either of you had with Rick—your homes, insurance, etcetera. All I ask is that we let this whole media circus die down, stop with the interviews, and responding to the allegations. I'm not asking you to sign anything, just simply give your word. None of us deserve this and even if Rick didn't mean for any of this to happen, it's his fault that it has. He's the only one who had all the information while we were in the dark." I exhaled. "All I can do is ask that we not reduce ourselves to women fighting over a man. That's it."

I waited for either of them to say something.

"I don't have a problem with that," Iris finally said.

We both turned to Amy.

"Is this the death certificate?" She picked up the envelope at the center of the table with her name on it.

"Yes, it's yours to take," I answered.

"If that's it, I'll be on my way." She picked up her purse and backed her chair away from the table.

"I know you're angry, Amy, but try to find forgiveness in your heart—for Ricky and this whole situation. You're not the only one humiliated here."

Amy stood, sucked in a deep breath, and stepped to the door, never turning back.

"Well, that's that, I guess," I mumbled. "There's really nothing else, Iris. Here's your copy of the death certificate." I handed her the other envelope. "Please, let me know if there's anything further I can do. Take good care of your children."

"Thank you, Rose. I appreciate everything you've done and as disappointed as I am that the verdict didn't go my way, it could've been worse. I'm not even sure if I would've been as gracious as you've been."

The two of us hugged and she slipped through the doors, turning to wave as she left.

I hoped it wouldn't be the last I heard from her or Amy. I really wanted to keep up with how Rick's children were doing but I knew I had no control over that. I just prayed that Amy and Iris would honor our husband in that way.

Twenty-Three

Iris
One Year Later

I latched on...

*A*s usual, the media eventually turned its focus to some other unfortunate souls, so things turned back to basically normal. There were a few who wanted to drag me back to the nightmare but mostly people no longer cared. It wasn't a problem for me to move on and turn my grief and misfortune into a lucrative business opportunity. My own notoriety increased due to the scandal, so several offers came my way. I latched on to a couple of them. That's what strong women do—with God's help, of course, and the motivation of taking care of small children.

Because Rose had admonished me to stop being so public with the fiasco Erick left behind, I did ask for her blessings to use our public misfortune as a platform for a talk show. One year later, a pilot show was created and shot focusing on bigamy and cheating spouses—infidelity in general. I felt I owed her that just for her simple kindness. It pays well, and I plan to ride the wave because I know all talk shows have an expiration date. And then, I'll be on to some other opportunity.

Initially, I was hot as hell that I didn't win the case. After all, I was the last to marry Erick and we had a young new family. During the proceedings I clung to the love I knew he had for us and was confident things would go my way. Once things died down, and after that meeting with Rose at her attorney's office, I calmed down. The only thing that made me feel better about not winning was Rose winning and knowing she could be counted on to be fair. With all the fighting between Amy and me, it was obvious the Universe was teaching us a lesson. Well, I learned it and made the decision to move on with life.

Many friends and associates have tried hooking me up on dates but for now, my heart is still in the past. I haven't met a man that has me interested enough to move on just yet. Who could ever compete with the life-saving doctor? I often wonder if Rose and Amy feel the same way.

I still haven't spoken to hateful Amy, but I hear she hasn't let any grass grow under her feet. She moved away, and I imagine she's somewhere passing. What should've happened was that we all came together for the sake of the children. I guess when Jersey and Darius are older, I'll tell them about their sister and brother and maybe the four of them can come together, love and look out for one a-nother. I hope.

Twenty-Four

Amy

I no longer worried…

$\mathcal{I}$ sold the family home and trekked to Florida. With my insurance money, I bought a small condo not far from the beach, and finally using my degree, working full time as a librarian at a library a few miles north of the ocean's shore. I was all too happy to leave the desert heat of Texas for the temperate warmth and sounds of the ocean waves within earshot. My only regret was that I hadn't done it sooner.

I was so stuck to the life I had with Ricky that I couldn't see that he'd had no problem making several other lives for himself. Most days I love and miss him and then there are other days that I can't believe that, even with all of his faults and his cheating, I was duped by the man I thought loved only me. Finding out about Rose and Iris, and how he had created real lives with each of them, was some reality for my ass. But, life goes on.

I date sometimes and have enjoyed that very much. I feel free, finally. I never spoke with David again after he lied in court. I wanted to ask him why, but I chalked it up to him being mad that I'd disappeared when Ricky died. Who knows why he did that. Or, maybe he thought he was telling the truth. Either way, I wasn't going to give him the satisfaction of thinking I cared enough to ask.

My children and I are in the same state—close enough for me, yet far enough for them. Ricky did a good job of planning for Kory and Kylie and really, that was all I wanted. I no longer worried about Rose or Iris taking anything from them. I'm sure Rose wanted me to bow down and kiss her feet for giving me a copy of the death certificate but Ricky belonged to me first, so why would I thank her for what was rightfully mine?

I was so happy to leave Texas—Rose and Iris—behind. As much as possible, I act like none of it ever happened. The only thing we had in common was Ricky so there was no need in trying to maintain any other type of relationship. I don't wish anything bad on them—I just wish them gone.

Elaine FLOWERS

is a professional writer of mainstream fiction residing in Dallas, Texas. She became a published author in 2004 with the release of her *Dallas Morning News* bestselling novel, "Black Beauty" and went on to pen seven more books.

FLOWERS' current book is on the woes of dating in the 21st century titled, **"MGTOW: Ten Things Men Don't Do Anymore"** derived from her blog on dating.

FLOWERS holds a Bachelors of Fine Arts in Creative Writing for Entertainment from Full Sail University and is also a book editor and book publisher.

BooksByElaineFlowers.com

BeforeYouPublish Book Press™
—— We Publish Books ——

BEFOREYOUPUBLISH.COM